THERE'S AN APP FOR THAT

Paddy Kelly

THERE'S AN APP FOR THAT

FICTION4ALL

DEDICATION

This work is dedicated to

Three Crazy Sisters:

Funny Face, Boo Boo & Hatti

May their lives be blessed with an absence of politics.

6

CONTENTS

INTRODUCTION TO APP ONE

Awareness of who, what, where, and most importantly why, we are is the driving force behind human existence.

In the following pages politics, religion and science will be discussed at various levels and opinions with which you may or may not agree. It is also possible that some of this may help you form, or at least solidify, some of your own opinions on these topics.

While science strives to shed ever more light on the answers to these questions, who, what, where and why, the ages old religious establishments, which have successfully leached onto and woven themselves into the political fabric of every nation on earth and therefore wield a disproportionate force of power then they have rightfully earned, strive to turn back the clock and frustrate the gains of honest men.

Most people agree that there are two things, religion and politics, that you shouldn't discuss in mixed company at dinners etc. . . But you never hear anyone say; "Now when we get to the Hendersons, don't bring up science!" It's always don't bring up religion or politics. Which I normally did . . . which is probably why I'm not still married, but let's not open up that old wound! The point is nobody ever says 'don't bring up science' because most people are not science literate.

If you've never heard this said about politics and religion, then you're probably too young to appreciate these essays. For those of you who fit this category think about it as the arguments for and against Apple and Mac only on steroids and where seven billion plus lives are at stake.

No pressure mind you.

The question that then arises is that given we need 'leaders' and both our political and religious leaders have continually lied, misled and betrayed us who do we 'trust' in so far as the word trust still retains any semblance of its traditional meaning?

Well, until they attempt to become politicians or religious fanatics, we trust the scientists. Not the political organizations with a powerful political lobby any of them represent or who are founded on political goals or purport to gather huge fortunes for 'research' in areas such as cancer.

I'm talking about the guys whose primary goal in life is the search for knowledge, the people commonly referred to as the 'pure' scientists. The guys in the trenches. The guys who get up in the morning and show up at the labs, the remote research sites or the classrooms and work through the day and many times into and through the night to fight to get one step closer to obtain some data that some other scientist can apply, use and discover one more thing that will bring us close to the facts and one step further from the myths, monsters and magical men people have 'believed' in for far too long.

And remember, while the suffix -ology denotes the scientific study of something, prefixing it with 'scient' doesn't make it scientific. Or real for that matter.

The other topic in this handful of short stories and essays, besides science and religion, is the other forbidden subject, politics.

Abuse of the English lexicon, largely by those in politics, has led to a significant chunk of our language being reduced to a hollow meaningless vocabulary.

Words such as equal, solemn promise and dedication when now used, particularly by the political elite, answer the question, "How do you know when a politician is lying?"

"His mouth is moving."

These writings are intended to be observational in nature with some opinion thrown in for flavor, opinion with which you may or may not agree. If you agree, thank you, if not; write your own book.

Thank you for taking the time to have a look at this and I hope you enjoy the read.

P. Kelly

FRIDAY MORNING

(First published in June, 2010)

It was a Friday morning chilly but not cold. Christmas was a month away.

In those days, in order to snag the night shift workers, bus and truck drivers, heading home from the factories and garages the bars didn't close.

Jimmy's Tavern sat on the corner of Delaware Street and Duncan Avenue in the center of a Jersey City, working class Irish-Italian neighborhood.

I was eleven and I was supposed to be in school but shining shoes was a hell of a lot more lucrative. Besides, the last person those sadistic old nuns at St. Aloysius were gonna miss was me. On top of which Friday was a language day which meant Mrs. LaFredo goose stepping up and down the aisles, arms folded above a bosom that could feed half the kids in Uganda, making us recite French phrases we'd use out in the street only if we had an overwhelming urge to get our ass kicked. With her Bouffant, beehive hair-do, size double D's, an ass that could hold a guy's drink while he danced with her all supported by a pair of legs that looked like they were nicked from the chop stick dispenser of a Chinese all-you-can-eat buffet, the little gutter snipes, bastards and assholes she taught, (us), called her 'cartoon lady'.

I never learned one lick of French but I liked Mrs. Lafredo. She probably never realized that she was a petunia struggling to grow in the middle of a

12

rugby pitch.

Apparently there was a standard recommended bar and tavern floor plan set out years prior by the East Coast Bar & Tavern Association of America because every bar I have ever been in before or since that day, had the long bar with a long line of stools in front of it set off to the right with tables and or booths to the left and the toilets located in the far rear of the room.

Jimmy's, one of the first joints in the neighborhood to have a TV, a little 24 inch job which was tucked away up in the far right hand corner mounted on a shelf turned at 45 degrees to the room and tilted down to the bar.

There was the usual sandwich bar set up on a large, stainless steel, roll-a-way food cart off to the left corner in the rear. First thing to catch my attention when I had entered the dark, smoky bar room which reeked of hops, smoke and sweat.

We all have a seminal incident when we first become 'aware' of the world around us, the outside world. Something outside our little Golden Triangular world of home-school-play.

That Friday morning was my moment of awakening.

Without warning somebody at the bar started yelling; "SHUT UP! EVERYBODY, SHUT THE HELL UP!" The bar man scurried to the television stepped up on the foot stool and turned the sound up. The black and white CBS announcer continued his running commentary and an eerie silence blanketed the shadowy bar room.

The man who saved us all from the devastation

of nuclear war during the Cuban Missile Crisis just a few weeks earlier, the guy who promised us we'd be on the moon by the end of the decade and the guy who almost restored people's faith in politics was dead. Shot in the head by a mad man in Texas.

Assassinations didn't happen in America, they were something that happened in far away Third World countries with strange names. Places where people got their water from wells and had exotic diseases that couldn't be cured and worse yet had no McDonalds.

Looking back on that exact moment I now realize what it must be like the first time the doctor tells you you have the Big C or some other fucked-up thing they're working on a cure for but it won't be ready in time to do you any good so bottom line is, your ride is here.

The standard American way to deal with something you couldn't deal with had finally reached the national level on a broad scale. Typical American philosophy. Can't deal with it, then apply canine reasoning, that is think like a dog. If you can't eat it or fuck it, kill it. Only difference is humans have guns. Makes killing much more efficient. You know, the difference between modern man and a caveman. A Caveman can only kill one person at a time.

Little did America realize that this was the start of an epidemic. Assassinations became fashionable after the Sixties, for both sides Cops and Criminals. What the hell? They got away with dusting the president, that means anybody can do it.

Something that went unnoticed and

unmentioned at the time was the irreversible effect the JFK assassination would have on the of national politics. Because of the nearly unlimited television coverage of the incident the realization that there was no safe haven for anyone anywhere in America, the U.S. public came just a little closer to that overwhelming, all consuming uncontrollable soup of paranoia they live in today, day in day out.

Fear of the unknown had already regularly manifested itself in the U.S. throughout its history. Fear of too many foreigners coming to their shores. Fear of the Nazi saboteurs that didn't exist during WWII. Fear of all the communists that people were told were in their government which didn't exist.

Odd that Americans have never developed a healthy fear of trusting their political leaders no matter how many times those leaders have cheated lied and stole from those who elected them.

People still rally behind these mysterious men who one day seem to appear out of nowhere with plenty of money to back them, slogans and promises and good hair. No matter what the fallout, what the damage four years later, the process starts all over again with new faces, new promises new coffers of cash to back them and Americans let themselves get sucked into the cult of political personalities as if they were internationally famous film stars who had just released a blockbuster, Oscar nominated feature destined to be a classic.

The conspiracy theories about who dusted JFK and why will persist as long as the event is remembered but two things are certain.

There were at the time really only two

organizations that were qualified or had the ability to pull such a thing off in the way it was executed at that level, both with the same quality of resources, inside intelligence and expertise.

For what it's worth, years later I sat in that sixth floor window in the Dallas School Book Depository two separate times, when, in classic tourist attraction fashion, it was set up with simulated crates and a fake rifle with a scope and tourists could look through before protests were apparently lodged and they blocked it all off.

Additionally I've made similar shots at 500 meters, twice the distance Oswald did, with similar weapons and while I was an expert marksman, I hold the same exact qualifications that Lee Harvey held. There can be no credible argument against the fact that Oswald did it, the question is did he set it up alone or with help? Probably with help.

Any argument concerning who did it and why is purely academic. The people will find out one day but because the politicians involved or those who had first-hand knowledge of the killing cleverly had key information sealed for in indeterminate period of time, when the truth is finally revealed the people it was relevant to will all be gone.

So just as we found out Teddy Roosevelt didn't charge up San Juan Hill, Churchill did have reliable knowledge of the attack on Pearl Harbor and nobody was burnt at the stake in Salem we'll one day find out the story behind the JFK assassination.

The two primary organizations with the ability to pull off the killing at the time were The U.S.

Government and the Mafia. Conspiracy theorists have feasted on this for years until it became a culturally imbedded joke.

Then came 9/11.

THE END

THE CESSATION OF DISCONTINUANCE

(First published in June, 2010)

"It's the 95% dishonest politicians that are giving the rest of us a bad name!"

Garry Trudeau
Cartoonist

I just finished reading Gene Kerrigan's *Never Make A Promise You Can't Break* and would now like to share some thoughts spurred on by Gene's insightful look at the delightful world of politics.

I am mostly known as a novelist, but I would like to take steps to rectify this. It is common knowledge that I left Ireland at an early age and went to America. What is not well known is that my ambitions in the States were never fully realized, that is to become a stalwart, honest, upright politician following in the footsteps of such legends as Gerald Ford, George Bush, Bill Clinton and who can forget what's-his-name? The peanut farmer. . . Carter! After obtaining citizenship in the States, I applied to be a politician.

However, I was told I was "technically ineligible", as my parents were married at the time. This of course came as a great shock to me. So in lieu of becoming a stand-up guy, I became a writer.

Now that I'm staging a comeback as a

politician I have plans to resuscitate old, long dead ambitions and would like to use Mr. Kerrigan's guidance to hone up on my public speaking and rhetoric abilities in order to prepare for my upcoming campaign.

To this end I have chosen a suitably controversial subject on which to voice my opinion and take a clear stance, not unlike my heroes and the superlative way in which they dealt with the subjects of police brutality in America, the budget deficit and Weapons of Mass Destruction, which have mysteriously vanished from the face of the earth, as they do. (Personally, I think they looked in the wrong place. Deep in the mountains of Montana would have been a good start).

Firstly, it is crucial to express how great it is to be back in New York City, the only place I know where everyone who knows how to run the country is driving taxi or running a pub. Consequently may I say how pleased I am with the current state of affairs in American politics, particularly the common punctuality of the public transport systems, the commendable level of transparency with which business is transacted in the halls of Congress and the un-Godly reasonable and stable price of essentials such as gas and groceries.

Some say, concerning issues like the one I am about to talk to you about, that it is harder to get at the facts than to get at the truth in a Congressional investigation, a task harder than doing Chinese arithmetic. Especially when another member of Congress is being 'investigated' wink, wink, nudge, nudge.

And to be perfectly clear, the issue to which I refer is not whether or not the U.S. military should remain in the Middle East or be deployed to the capitol during the next election. I would be loath to put our young men and women in such a potentially life threatening situation.

Then what is this issue you ask? Certainly it needs no introduction. It is an issue relevant to the entire population of this country. Especially those of us in the United States. An issue so controversial that few venture to take a clear stand on it. Let me just say that in this case, that is not the case. I am talking about an issue first recognized by the esteemed journalists everywhere including Gene Kerrigan, (q.v.). I am talking about The Cessation of Discontinuance.

After having consulted various experts on the subject of Cessation, such as the TMA people on cessation of timely transport and reasonable search, the folks from AT&T on the cessation of reasonable prices for roaming charges and the Clinton News Network and Bill O'Reilly on the cessation of intelligent commentary, I agree with Mr. Kerrigan that the inevitable conclusion is that the Cessation of Discontinuance is a step we cannot afford not to take.

So in the next round of rigged elections in 2016 vote 'Yes' if you mean No and 'No' if you mean Yes, and remember, this has been a paid political announcement from the GOC, the Government of and for the Corporations. The political party that **can** organize a piss up in a brewery.

THE END

THERE'S AN APP FOR THAT!
(First published in June, 2011)

Back in the early Eighties, (or the Late Walkman Age just before the Early DVD Age as they are now known in history and science texts), I had one of those leather bound bricks we euphemistically referred to as 'phones'. You know, the black plastic brick with the mini penis sticking out the top which came with a complimentary genuine, imitation leather phone condom to slip it into. The phones where you could almost, most of the time get a sometimes clear connection for one to two minutes at a stretch but had to carry judicially otherwise the bicep of your dominant arm would be twice the size of the other one inside of a month!

I was walking along Central Park West with my Zenith Black Brick model X21 in my left hand, (I'm right hand dominant), when I got a call. On a bench next to where I stopped to take it sat an old man in a Mets baseball cap and red flannel shirt, Farmer Brown jeans and work boots. He was easily in his 90's.

When the call was finished, due to solar flares affecting the relative trajectory of the earth's rotation secondary to Mars being in juxtaposition with Aries, I lost connection and the old man called me over.

"You a cop?" He grumbled.

"No." I responded not bothering to explain that I had in fact applied to the NYPD years prior but was declared ineligible. I would only shoot people who shot at me.

"Why?" I asked.

"You got a walkie-talkie. I thought maybe you was a cop!"

"This isn't a walkie-talkie. It's a phone."

"A PHONE?!" He gasped. I handed it to him and he examined it. "How far can you talk with this thing?" He grunted as he scanned it.

"Theoretically, with a sat-com connection, anywhere on earth." I informed him.

He cocked back his Mets baseball cap, fell back on the bench and the colour drained from his face. That's when it hit me. This guy was born before movies, television, even radio! The revelation that the world had come so far in his relatively short life time was a genuine shock to him.

I had a strong urge to sit and chat with that old guy but I was running late. I had to get to the phone repair store.

I've always had the impression that few people are aware of the age they're living in. The poor schmucks in the Middle Ages who suffered through the Plague, the 100 Years' War which dragged on for 116 years, the Inquisition or the Crusades or the invention of Boy Bands and Pop music were no doubt painfully aware of the times they were living in. But even the educated, for the most part, are not really 'aware' of the times they are living in.

Back at City University we had to take a course entitled 'Man and Technology'. Pre-meds, engineering and sociology students were all required to take it their senior year. The idea was to orient us, people who were going to make their living at dealing with people, about how people throughout time adjusted, or didn't adjust, to new technology.

It was taught by three professors, one from each discipline all at once, in an auditorium large enough to house my entire primary school.

Dr. George Kelly, the Biologist, never used the microphone, never needed it. He had served in Patton's Third Army, landed in Gela, Sicily in *Operation Husky*, fought at Anzio, all the way up the Italian peninsula and fought on into Germany and was in on the taking of Berlin. He was a combat medic when they used to close wounds on the battlefield with safety pins. He had been wounded himself, twice. Real world experience wasn't an issue.

Everyone knew his biog and he was well liked.

Dr. Ludcheck, an Eastern European civil engineer who had escaped the Nazis by travelling to the States truly believed the streets in America were paved with gold, all people were treated as equals and anyone could rise to fame and glory. In other words he bought into the program.

Dr. Manning was a right wing liberal who, sheltered by the university system from his first year in college, had never ventured outside and so had no clue of the real world. Any and all knowledge he had ever obtained about anything came from a book. But only certain books.

It was Manning's turn to start the show and the topic according to the syllabus was nuclear energy.

Dr. Manning took the podium, adjusted the mic

and opened his part of the three hour lecture.

"Nuclear energy, how has it been received by the public?" Kelly and Ludcheck took their seats at the back of the auditorium. "I would like to start my talk with the unnecessary bombings of Hiroshima and Nagasaki." He started

As if someone were shooting a Michael Jackson video, on the director's cue, the entire auditorium stopped writing, dropped their pens and looked up awaiting the ensuing attack. Also on cue the F4U Corsair strafing began, with Dr. George Kelly in the pilot's seat.

"NOW WAIT JUST A GOD DAMNED MINUTE THERE MANNING!" Kelly, flying down the center aisle, finger waving, yelling and with his long, white lab coat flapping behind him like Super Prof's cape was down in front of the podium in seconds ignoring Manning and holding court to the entire class.

"UNLIKE YOURSELF I FOUGHT IN THAT DAMN WAR AND WHEN WE FINISHED WITH THE NAZIS AND WERE TOLD WE WERE NOT GOING HOME BUT HAD TO PACK UP AND NOW GO FIGHT THE JAPANESE, I WAS GOD DAMNED GLAD THEY DROPPED THAT BOMB!"

Slightly more calmly George then proceeded to relate the casualty statistics he had personally encountered in the last two and half years of fighting and the estimated death stats they could be expected based on the battles which had been fought against the Japanese so far - in excess of one million Americans.

His emotionally induced tirade lasted a good ten minutes but being the gracious scientist he was Dr. George then apologized for his outburst and headed back up the aisle of the auditorium.

But there was no doubt about the temperature of the lecture hall.

As he retired back to his seat George got a rousing ten minute standing ovation from all 500 students replete with hooping, hollering and all sorts of other hillbilly styled expressions of support to the point that the eloquent old doctor of biology turned beet red with embarrassment and had to temporarily step outside the auditorium.

Manning readjusted himself at the podium, attempting to ignore the applause then spent about five minutes more reshuffling his notes discarding the first dozen pages or so and finally stuttered into a continuance.

"Well . . . obviously there are differing opinions. We shall now turn out attention to the Three Mile Island incident."

As with anything, it's all about perspective. People react to new technology in different lights.

A quarter of a century after the Central Park encounter, (only a few years in my void-of-time-parameters mind), after the old man on the bench incident I was in the lounge of the hotel where I lived with several other guests watching a DVD of the beer contest scene in the comedy film *Beer Fest* when a song came on that I had never heard but liked.

"Anybody know the name of that song?" I threw out to the room.

"Put it on hold." A cute little twenty-something said.

I always listen when cute little twenty-somethings speak, so I manned the remote.

She walked to the TV and asked me to press 'play', I did and she punched a few buttons and held her palm-sized phone up to the plasma screen for a few seconds, read the read out on the phone's screen and turned to me.

"That's Plastic Bertrand singing *Ce Plane Pour Moi*. It's French!" She gleefully informed and re-took her seat to which my mind instantly responded with:

"HOW THE FUCK . . . ?!"

I felt like I was 90 years old sitting on a park bench in Central Park with a cute little twenty-something educating me about 'Apps'.

Where's my Mets cap?

THE END

THE MASTER OF JERSEY CITY POLITICS

(First published in June, 2009)

"Politics is the art of excluding a man from affairs
which rightly concern him."

- Voltaire

Catholics have this primitive ritual they put
you through when you're seven years old.
The age is well considered, because any
older and you'd probably ask too many questions.
Or die laughing your ass off at the answers.

They dress you up in a nice new suit you'll
never use again, herd you along with a collection of
30 or 40 other scared shitless seven year olds into a
church, ask you a bunch of questions on things that
have been drilled into you for weeks on end
beforehand then they feed you a small, round piece
of bread. This now, you are told, washes you square
with God which came as a surprise because none of
us knew we were in Dutch with The Almighty but
afterwards we all felt pretty good about being back
on his good side.

They don't of course tell you it's only
temporary. Clever bastards.

Under the Catholic's somewhat detailed
legislation system, you were still required to confess
once a week whether you did anything or not.
Which in essence means you had to make shit up or
the priest wouldn't believe you. Which is a lie which

of course is a sin. Perhaps in lieu of a crucifix the logo for Catholicism should have been a gerbil running on a little wheel.

Too awkward to wear around the neck I suppose.

Born into this system, as he got older Butchie saw all this as a mandate to sin. After all, when you've got a bunch of gullible adults who think this whole plane of existence is nothing more than one big magic show being ring mastered by an old guy floating around up in the clouds, you feel somehow obligated to take advantage.

Pay no attention to that man behind the curtain.

Of course he had been cautioned by an older kid not to chew the little, round piece of bread when they put it in his mouth. Nun Radar screens all over the parish, Butchie was warned, would light up and eerily garbed, sexually frustrated, middle-aged females would be tripping over themselves to dish out whacks across the back of the head with wooden paddles, 18 inch rulers or in the case of Sister Mary Bull Dyke, the back of her ham hock-sized paw.

Clergy are your friend and getting punished is good.

An hour after the ceremony, he was home surrounded by friends he'd never knew he had and relatives he never wanted to know he had like the two hundred year old moustached aunt. Everyone was handing him envelopes with dollar bills neatly tucked into cards of congratulation of which he was only the temporary custodian as he knew they would become the possession of his mom as soon as the food and booze ran out and everybody high-

28

tailed it out the door and went home. The relatives who would inevitably be held in highest esteem were the ones whose envelopes contained something you might never have heard of or seen – a five dollar bill.

This whole thing was labelled "First Holy Communion", a reaffirmation of his Catholic life and how he was going to live it as a pious and holy person the rest of his days even though that meant as much to a seven year old as the words Budget Deficit, Cold War, Military Intelligence or Nuclear Fallout Shelter. Or any other number of oxymorons.

It was around this time that Butchie was unintentionally ushered into life in America by a short, slightly built, fidgety, Italian guy named Vincenzo Ferro whose friends called him Vinnie. He reminded Butchie of a dark haired Chihuahua that walked upright on its hind legs.

Not everyone knew Vinnie but Vinnie knew everyone. He was a Ward Boss in one of Jersey City's political ward districts back in the late Fifties and early Sixties. He showed up briefly at Butchie's First Holy Communion party, (First Holy Communion 'reception' if you lived north of The Heights), and handed him the obligatory envelope, gave congratulations and vanished. Later when the kid's mom opened it she nearly cried. There was a twenty inside. Groceries for a week.

Vinnie was a direct appointee of the Mayor, Thomas Gangemi. They were pisanos to the point that Vinnie could show up at the mayor's office and, ahead of several other visitors, be granted an audience with His Holiness within a couple of minutes.

This later would impress the hell out of Butchie.

In those days there was a temporary truce between the two most powerful factions in the greater New York-New Jersey area, the Italians and the Irish. Things were changing and unlike the days between Al Capone and Eddie O'Bannon in Chicago, survival instincts dictated that agreements had to be made, deals had to struck and contracts had to be signed. This worked out well for the holy fathers of the Catholic Church, as all the Guidos and all the Paddys were all Catholic.

Vinnie was a shoe-in with the Italians and actively courted the Irish ergo he had powerful friends on both sides. Key to both parties was the fact that Vinnie was in good with the Mayor.

Butchie's mother, being of Sicilian origin, had no qualms about her boy hanging out with the likes of an older male Italian politician, his fellow politicians and their associates, priests and Mafiosi. She figured they were all more or less from the same caste. How times have changed.

At least it's still okay for kids to hang out around Mafiosi.

Despite the fact he hadn't a clue what Ferro was talking about most of the time, to Butchie Vinnie was like a second father. He took pains to teach Butchie the rules of being a man. Rules like always look a man in the eye and nod hello when you pass him on the street. Despite the fact the kid was doing good just to look somebody in the crotch when he passed them on the street much less the eye, the kid

30

knew what he meant.

Another rule was that you never call elders by their first name. The fact that he insisted on Butchie calling him 'Vinnie' meant a lot.

"See him? Don't believe a word he says." Vinnie randomly advised as they walked down Duncan Avenue one crisp autumn day.

"Why not Vinnie?"

"He's Corsican! French are compulsive liars!" Vinnie spewed as they made their way through a dirty Jersey City alley and out onto the wide open spaces of West Side Avenue.

"Who's he?" Butchie asked without a clue why he asked but wanting to keep the one sided conversation going.

"He's a Republican! They're gonna fuck this country up one day!"

"What's a Republican?" Only five foot two and in spite of his shin-length, grey heavy, woollen overcoat with the herring bone pattern Ferro could still out walk a champion jogger. Butchie's days with him were a constant blend of scurrying to keep pace through the city streets punctuated by short respites in a bar, lounge or private ethnic club as they pin balled from place to place to do the covert business of not so small time, Jersey City politics.

"There are only two kinds of people, Democrats and Republicans." Vinnie preached.

"You mean there's nobody else?!"

"Nobody except the Commies, Hippies and left wing Liberals, but they're all the same."

"Which one are you?"

"I'm a Democrat."

31

"What's a Democrat?" The kid's words were pointed squarely up at Ferro's head while his eyes were zeroed in on the steaming calzones being placed in the window of Poluzzo's Pizzeria on the corner.

It was only half past ten in the a.m. but there would be considerable foot traffic for the next hour and a half and, as was usually the case, Butchie hadn't had any breakfast.

Unbeknownst to the kid, Vinnie knew this. Vinnie always knew this. Vinnie always knew everything. He's where Butchie learned the word omnipotent.

"The Democrats are the guys who fight to keep this country the great social experiment that it is. A place where everyone is equal no matter what."

"Then what's a Republican?"

"Somebody who when he talks you can always tell he's lying." This is a trick the kid wanted to know!

"How can you tell that?"

"His mouth's moving." Vinnie snarked.

***

They stopped about a block and a half up West Side Avenue and turned into a hundred year old store front which looked like it could have, at one time, served as a neighborhood grocers, a dry goods store or a bar. Both windows, which straddled the centrally located, recessed door, had been blocked out by dark green, velvet curtains as was the door's window. Small gold leaf lettering outlined in black

32

enamel at face height on the door read:

Inside slivers of the crisp autumn daylight leaked around the curtains to bathe the row of round tables down the left hand wall and neutralized what little color there was in the place while casting surrealistic shadows across the room-length bar dominating the right hand side of the long, narrow room.

Vinnie and the bar tender exchanged nods as he and the kid made their way straight through the endless room to another dark green curtain in the back. Butchie tried to stand as tall as possible as he traded nods with an old man sitting at one of the round tables reading *la Republica*. He scurried behind Ferro through the curtain and into the back room.

At a table in the back of the back room there was some kind of game in progress which was difficult to make out for the cloud of cigar and cigarette smoke. Vinnie peddled past the players calling them by name and veered off to the single booth in the left hand corner.

By now, Butchie knew the routine. After dragging one of the bentwood chairs within a few feet he drifted over to the gaming table to kill time, watch, learn and wait.

Though he had been there many times before he always enjoyed hanging around the club. Made

33

him feel like one of the guys. A grown up, not a schoolboy any more. The riggottzi always treated him like a man, never like a kid. They took him as serious as they took everyone else. Butchie didn't realize it at the time, but he had learned about the single most important attribute of human relationship.

He had learned about respect.

Although clueless as to what most of the men were talking about, he'd spend hours studying their ways, mannerisms and speech patterns. Even when they occasionally lapsed into English the vocabulary, much less the topics, were essentially incomprehensible, but the meanings were crystal clear.

That and he liked the club because he always liked stepping back in time to the Nineteenth Century. All around him lay the dark, pungent, smoky, bar room. This was Man-Central! A gallon puddle of estrogen in here would evaporate faster than if spilled on the surface of the sun. If some careless rigottzo knocked over a drink there was no scorn or derision heaped on him propagated by a misconception of the war of the sexes. He might be the brunt of a manly joke as the bar man calmly pulled another glass for him knowing the client would not only happily pay for another but the tender would get a tip when the client was ready to leave.

This was a refuge where men could vent about their women to the same degree that women could bitch about their men in the kitchen, at a Tupperware party or over cocktails in a lounge somewhere with the girls.

A perfect commune of the Yang to compliment the Ying.

After half an hour or so, Butchie had no sense of time back then, a thick envelope was pushed across the table where it would wait until the men stood, hugged, traded kisses on the cheeks, shook hands and uttered what was his first exposure to a foreign language. Italian.

"Mille grazie, pisano! Cunsider it done!"

After several hours of kibitzing about town, surreptitious meetings where Ferro would collect manila envelopes of varying thicknesses and meetings and where the men met in dark places and spoke in hushed tones alternating between English and Sicilian, came Butchie's favorite time of day, lunch. Which meant pizza! Pizza, the life blood of Western civilization.

Back out on the chilly streets the lesson continued.

"Vinnie?"

"Yeah Kid?"

"Could I axe you a question?"

"Sure Kid, what is it?"

"What's in all them vanilla envelopes?"

"Ma-nila envelopes." He corrected. "Just papers Kid. Important papers."

Glancing at his gold Rolex, Vinnie'd always ask; "What'a ya suppose we should do for lunch, Kid?" Knowing the answer he'd ask anyway. Without waiting for an answer he'd suddenly remember he had business at some undisclosed location which required them to go past Joey's,

Jersey City's pre-eminent Pizzeria on Journal Square.

"Ahh, what the hell? We gotta go that way anyways!" Vinnie would reason.

Strange that Vinnie never ate pizza.

Joey Capone, a first cousin of Al whose family was driven out of Chicago by the same rival gang that got Al Capone, the Feds, was intended by God to be Bud Abbot's partner in comedy Lou Costello. Physically he was a dead ringer for the comic actor. There was no end to jokes to this effect and Joey never varied in his comeback in response to such mockery.

"Fuckin' never fuckin' gets old. Know-what-I-fuckin'-mean?"

Joey's, or more formally *Joey's Pizza*, was laid out according to the U.S. East Coast Pizzeria's Universal Floor Plan Regulations. Two tiered pizza oven behind a tall serving counter to the right as you walked in, a row of booths down the left hand side, ending even with the far edge of the counter and from there back to the toilets the remaining floor space sported four-top tables and bentwood chairs. Each table had, arranged in perfect size order, one chrome napkin dispenser, one salt shaker, one pepper shaker, one round parmesano cheese dispenser, complete with six day old parmesano cheese and one laminated, four sided menu with an impressionistic two color print of Venetian gondolas paddling serene lovers through a canal off into the sunset.

The only other item was a Mateus wine bottle with a partially melted red candle jammed in the top with just enough melted wax dribbled down the sides of the bottle to add ambience.

No cheesy red and white checkered table clothes or ketchup bottles on the tables for Joey's place! His place was pure class.

It was on one of their lunchtime forays that it occurred. The crime of the century that, to this day, remains unsolved. The great Jersey City mozzarella heist.

Butchie was at a table in the back of the place attacking a hot slice of margarita with a second standing by to fill in as soon as needed with a Nehi root beer for back-up. Vinnie was in a booth up front talking to Joey the owner when the commotion started.

It was just after noon when the phone rang and Joey excused himself, left Vinnie with his third espresso and went to answer it. What has to be the shortest phone conversation on record then ensued after which Joey quickly hung up and proceeded to quietly go table to table and ask the half dozen patrons to leave the restaurant. Naturally some objected but the promise of a full three course dinner for two any night next week placated even the most obstinate protesters.

Joey nodded at Vinnie who signalled to the kid which he took to mean, 'just keep eating'.

No fuckin' argument there.

Joey scurried after the last customers to leave, locked the doors and lowered the window shades. Minutes later, not knowing what was about to happen as Butchie dug into his second slice to get it down quickly, just in case the shooting started, there was a knock at the back door.

As Joey ran to answer it he ripped open the walk-in cooler to his right in the back which stood just inside the rear door.

Three rough looking Pisos hurriedly entered, each carrying a four foot long loaf of fresh mozzarella. It was obviously not their first time in the place as they went straight for the walk-in and for the next five minutes, like a mini-assembly line, loaves of fresh mozzarella were brought in and hung up inside the fridge.

As quickly as they had appeared they were gone and a minute later the shades were up, the back door was locked, the front door was opened and *Joey's* was once again open for trade and some poor bastard somewhere was filling out a police report to take to an insurance company for his missing cheese.

"Can you describe the cheese sir? When was the cheese last seen? Have you noticed any unusually large rodents in the neighborhood recently? Is it possible you could work with one of our police sketch artists so we can get a better picture of the missing mozzarella?"

Life went on.

***

United Steel Workers
Local #871
Union Hall

After their usual lunch of pizza it was back to

38

business.

In the course of their zig-zagging across and through the city, the bars, the halls and quite a few palatial, private homes which were for some reason all dark and smoky like a throwback to Victorian times, they came on their next destination. No matter how plain or elaborate, lighting seemed to be subdued at best in all these places. In addition to which everyone over the age of fifteen seemed to smoke.

Despite the early afternoon hour the Steel Workers Union Hall, Local 871, on Jackson Avenue was dark. Dark and smoky. Like the multitude of bars they had visited in the months since Butchie had become Vinnie's surrogate offspring there was considerable activity.

This afternoon there was a Democratic Party fund raiser underway and thanks largely to the free food and beer, the large, open hall was packed.

Butchie followed Vinnie through the milling crowd and around back of the stage area where he met and was greeted warmly by some very important looking people. Whenever the really important looking guy, the eldest and fattest in the group of about half a dozen moved, the two most pugnacious looking guys shadowed him. As one reached out his hand to be introduced to Vinnie the .45 Colt in his shoulder holster became partially visible.

As the elaborate Italian introductions went on Butchie's attention was caught by the ten foot tall, drunk bagpiper in full Highland regalia who, as he was putting on his Gilley brogues tipped slowly but ever more backwards, each time catching himself at the last minute until his luck ran out. He finally challenged the gravity barrier one too many times and slipped from the low bench crashing to the floor.

No one in the crowded back room but Butchie seemed to pay attention as the Highlander climbed back to his feet, regained himself, manned his pipes and shifted to the back stage door leading out to the main room.

Less than a minute later he was marching out onto the hall's stage, driving the crowd crazy with *Scotland the Brave*.

The massive amounts of food over at the mile and a half long buffet were the next distraction and Butchie's radar soon related longitudes and latitudes to his wheel house. He set course accordingly. It was once again, a blatant reminder of why he took to spending so much time away from home. Food! For some strange reason there was never any at home but everywhere he went with Ferro . . .

Butchie went to work engineering a pair of sandwiches, (always planning ahead, one for later), which some say would later serve as inspiration for the modification in the World Trade Center design. There was originally only supposed to be one.

Butchie could not have cared less that someone somewhere in the room had had one too many and words were being exchanged. Minutes later the shoving contest was unsuccessfully intervened with and graduated to an exchange of fists. By the time furniture started flying, Butchie, his Dagwoods stashed lovingly in a red cloth napkin, braved the no man's land back to where he left Vinnie and at the sound of the first siren Ferro hustled the two of them out the back door of the hall and to sanctuary in the known, friendly environs of Jackson Avenue.

***

"The Brawl in the Hall" as it was billed in the local Press, quickly faded from the headlines as a new, much more serious and wide spread issue insidiously spread and suddenly exploded onto the social scene of Jersey City, New Jersey.

The brawl between the races.

With the cooperation of the Catholic Church, politicians and payoffs the Irish and the Italians had learned to live together. There were after all certain European cultural standards the two shared.

To the most recent immigrants to this three hundred and fifty year old neighbourhood however, the blacks, everybody who wasn't black was white. There were no Irish, Italians, Poles or Hungarians. Not even Micks, Wops, Pollocks or Kikes. Just whites. In a very short period of time this quickly deteriorated into all whites being referred to by what was originally the racially derogatory term for Hungarians, 'Honkies'. Later this became 'Whitey' before being elevated to 'Cracker'.

Having lost their native cultures centuries prior the blacks never really understood culturally based conflicts as they existed between the Irish and Italians for example. Not fitting in to the social structure they choose to currently inhabit, naturally turned up the pressure in their own communities.

41

One day as they turned the corner onto Pine Street, coming from lunch enroute to the Italian American Club, Butchie and Vinnie spotted a common neighborhood visitor. A pair of white, Cadillac ambulances, red roof lights flashing away, were parked outside what used to be a Georgian house turned Brown Stone Walk-up now converted into a low rent apartment house.

Ambulance attendants were evacuating two casualties, both black men, while two police officers were handcuffing two women.

One of the blood soaked men, a large tag of flesh flapping from his face in rhythm as he limped down the long set of granite steps outside the front entrance, was being held up by one ambulance attendant, his white shirt and trousers also saturated in blood from the man's multiple stab and slash wounds. The second casualty was being carried down the steps of the tall front porch on a stretcher, covered in a blood-soaked, linen sheet. A fourth attendant dutifully trailed behind, carrying a severed arm eloquently dressed in a formerly white cotton shirt with a gold cufflink. One of the cops had a blood stained butcher knife and a large cleaver taking both out to the car with the women, apparently as evidence.

"Ba fongulo!" Vinnie softly whispered.

A neighbor was relating to the other cop that the two men were playing cards when an argument erupted, and it deteriorated into a punch up, during which the two women faithfully armed their men.

As they watched a fourth ambulance attendant place the blood dripping, severed arm on the stretcher with the dying man, a by-stander casually commented.

"Musta' bin playin' fo' money."

A short time later, after the ambulances drove off and the cops and rubber neckers had gone about their business, the two silently stared down as they circumvented the crusted over puddle of blood on the sidewalk. They left the elderly Jewish landlady to her scrubbing of the front steps and journeyed on.

It was a little ways down the street that for Butchie, everything came screaming into focus. The logic and perspective of the blacks, as well as the basis for all American society, was immediately crystal clear.

No less than in any African nation or Asian Third World country, violence in the U.S. was a way of life.

Particularly where money was involved.

***

It was in late September of 1963, Butchie was eleven, and Thomas Gangemi was mayor.

As had been Gangem's habit throughout his tenure, four or five nights a week the Mayor 'held court' in *il Vento's Italian Restaurant* on West Side Avenue.

In keeping with Italian tradition he used the high profile eatery as a de facto, after-hours office granting audiences to minor as well as major suitors who would come to patronize the current Godfather of the city. In between drinks, cavorting over city business, drinks, dinner and drinks he would hear all manner of petitions.

The former Godfather, retired mayor John V. Kenny alias "The Little Guy", now at the advanced age of 70 was the man who had actually established the current hierarchy just after the Second World War over which Gangemi now ruled.

By unwritten but religiously adhered to tradition, the older Godfathers were universally respected and wielded considerable influence.

That Sunday evening the older, diminutive Kenny showed up, unscheduled, in the middle of a court session. Without so much as a greeting, Gangemi ignored him and carried on with his bullshit session.

Kenny approached and informed Gangemi that he had some documents he'd like Gangemi to look at.

"Sit down, I'll see you when I'm ready."

"But-"

"I said sit, I'll be with you in a minute!"

Silence prevailed over the small gathering at the overt breach of gangland protocol.

Kenny didn't respond, only quietly stepped aside and took a seat in a corner booth, facing out, one elbow on the table. The now not-so-important papers in hand.

That's right, you're the Mayor now. Kenny quietly mumbled to the floor.

Back at the Mayor's table the tone of the conversation had noticeably altered and become more subdued.

Gangemi himself showed signs of nervousness as it slowly dawned on him that just maybe he let his Italian temper get the better of him.

After a short time Gangemi called over to Kenny and asked to see the documents. Kenny, without a word, pushed up from the seat, crossed the floor and handed him the folder.

Gangemi thumbed through the papers, gave his approval and returned the folder along with a half-hearted apology for making Kenny wait. Kenny nodded and without a word, made for the door.

There was no shortage of speculation the following day as the Jersey City rumor mill cranked into overtime with reports of the incident.

Two days later, on Tuesday morning, a certified letter by private carrier arrived at the Mayor's office.

The Feds had somehow received information proving that Gangemi was born in Italy and had never applied for or received U.S. citizenship.

The mayor was an illegal alien.

That Wednesday morning, September 25th, 1963 Thomas Gangemi was forced to resign as thirty-fifth head of the most lucrative legally corrupt branch of organized crime in the United States; Mayor of Jersey City, New Jersey.

From that point on the Feds were camped out in Jersey City.

***

About a week later Butchie got to Vinnie's ground floor apartment one Wednesday afternoon, right after school. He always got a laugh out of watching the little man wash up, shave and brush his teeth with the same yellow bar of Dial soap.

When he let himself in there were two men in suits sitting on the couch. Big men with greying hair who apparently didn't know how to smile. Or perhaps had forgotten how. They both wore fedoras and heavy overcoats. One of the overcoats hung open and he could see a gun under the man's arm. Vinnie came out of the bathroom smiling as he dried his face.

"We can't visit today Butchie. I gotta go with these men."

Butchie had no clue what was happening but knew it wasn't good as he watched Vinnie put on his long grey, overcoat, the one with the herring bone pattern and leave with the men. He followed them outside and was shocked at what he saw.

There were a couple of black and white squad cars, a Paddy wagon and a gaggle of press. Cameras were popping off all over the place and several reporters shouting questions added to the feeding frenzy.

Butchie watched intently as the face of his surrogate father faded into the shadows and the doors of the police Paddy wagon were closed over.

A handcuffed Vinnie smiled and waved at him through the barred doors as if he were going off on a holiday and not off to prison for the rest of his life where he would die.

***

After the Italians had their shot with the illegally elected Gangemi as mayor of Jersey City the Irish had their turn again.

It was eight years after Gangemi was out of the picture and the renowned hero and WWII bomber pilot Tommy Whelan was at the helm as mayor.

By now Butchie was finishing up high school at William L. Dickinson and had been offered an athletic scholarship to City University New York on the other side of the Hudson River and Jersey City had turned a corner. Or so most thought.

As the saying goes, ya can't teach an old whore new tricks and little had changed in Jersey City. Plus the Feds were still hovering.

A month after Butchie graduated high school at Dickinson in June of 1971 The Feds busted everyone in the Mayor's office.

Also that July the twice elected Whelan was indicted, convicted and given fifteen years in a Federal penitentiary by the U.S. Attorney's office as the senior member of the famous "Hudson County Eight" in a massive conspiracy and extortion case revolving around construction contract kickbacks worth millions.

The former Mayor, "The Little Guy", John V. Kenny, was also convicted in a separate Federal trial but died a few years later of a heart attack.

The following year the same Federal probe reached William L. Dickinson High and the school was closed for investigation of widespread sexual relations and drug sales between teachers and students.

Jersey City held numerous distinctions as a city

not least of which was serving as the primary operating grounds for most of The Mafia's trucking and shipping crimes and, coincidentally the William L. Dickinson High School had the honor of being the first and only U.S. high school to be investigated, taken over and closed by the Federal Department of Education, a cabinet level office which came about by laws largely founded on the evolution of what Dickinson had become and the numerous prosecutions which followed its closure.

The criminal charges? As they say in medical parlance, TNTC, Too Numerous To Count.

Apparently topping the popularity chart of illicit activity at the school was teachers buying drugs from students, gang violence and teachers selling drugs to students. Teachers engaging in frequent sexual activity with students, cooperation with local bookies for betting on high school football games and students engaging in frequent sexual activity with teachers, (on and off school grounds). Teachers helping students cheat on exams and the proverbial last straw, something involving the football team and a mature sheep.

This last one may sound worse than it actually was as the school's mascot was, after all, a ram.

Go Rams!

To their credit, at the week-long federal hearings in D.C. which ensued, the teachers vehemently denied ever helping students cheat on exams. Even teachers have their limits.

I never saw Vinnie again, but I guess I got out just in time.

Mom always said, "Due faccia della stessa

48

medaglia!" Crime and politics, two sides of the same coin.

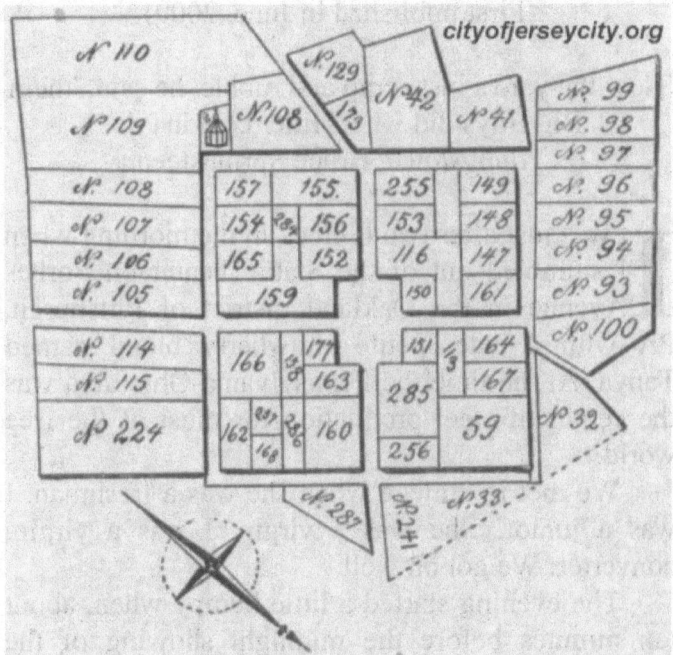

Jersey City plot plan circa 1660 A.D.

THE END

SELF-INDULGENCE & DENIAL IN PITTSBURGH

(First published in June, 2009)

'Now the yard's just scrap and rubble, he said, 'them
Big Boys did what Hitler couldn't do.'
Youngstown, Bruce Springsteen

It was just after two o'clock in the morning when I stumbled out of the State Theater on Forbes Avenue in the Oakland district of Pittsburgh, PA with a cute, petite strawberry blond named Tanya. At the time the Pennsylvania-Ohio area was the center of steel production for most of the free world.

We met in college when she was a freshman. I was a junior. She was a virgin. I was a virgin, converter. We got on well.

The evening started a little bumpy when, about ten minutes before the midnight showing of the *Rocky Horror Picture Show*, I looked past my date to spot what looked to be a ten year old boy at the other end of the row helping an overweight, balding guy, maybe 40, adjust his seating then watched as the old man leaned over and went to sleep. I nudged Tanya and said, "This guy thinks he's gonna sleep through this movie!"

With no hesitation the kid leaned forward and yelled back over to me, "He's blind!"

I always was pretty good at giving a good first impression.

In my defense I didn't know you weren't supposed to drink Irish whiskey after you dropped purple micro dot before going to the midnight movies.

A couple of hours later Tanya and I, along with about 600 other crazies, that warm Summer's evening, with nothing better to do while looking for direction in our rudderless lives, had just watched *The Rocky Horror Picture Show*. Richard O'Brien's astounding unclassifiable film had yet to reach world-wide success but it was the hippest hip phenomenon at the time. Largely because it hadn't yet become universally hip.

However, lurking in the shadows of despair was the bad news that the Japanese were about to pull the rug out from under us. Pearl Harbor didn't work out so well for them so they decided to get us with improved gas mileage.

Yes, the pride of western capitalism everywhere was about to be flushed down the shitter like a gastrically digested and processed Foot Long Chili Dog with cheese and a large order of fries fresh from the Big O!

The Big O Restaurant, right there on Forbes Avenue, was where we now found ourselves. Not the entire 600 members of the audience, but most of them jammed into that thirty-five seat, fast food joint with several, rotating metal stools sprouting from the white tiled floor lined up in front of the dinged up green, imitation marble counter.

With a pretty good buzz kicking in as I peered over the heads, (or from my 5'7" stunted P.O.V. **between** the heads of the mob), I watched the intense focus and concentration of the three young men behind the counter as they strove, (strived? striven?), to turn the seven loaves and five fish into enough to feed the masses.

Penis shaped dogs seemed to fly off the grill, sometimes two and three at a time, and gracefully land comfortably between the wide open, gaping halves of spread, steamy, white virgin, buns only seconds before various condiments appeared and gently oozed and bathed over said slightly seared savory sausages.

Sexual innuendos aside, grub and greenbacks changed hands at an impressive rate down at the end over the white Formica counter which held the register while the fed crowd undulated out through the narrow door spilling along the side streets sometimes blocking what little traffic there was as the hungry crowd members ebbed into and up to the marble alter. It was rush hour in the Manhattan IRT except with food minus the screeching, steel wheels and everybody was happy and under thirty.

An argument started out on the avenue when some cantankerous son-of-a-bitch decided his over-sized Dodge Dart was being purposely held up by the crowd until two good looking co-eds from the university sashayed over and offered to share their food with him. Poor hard hat orientated bastard never stood a chance. As a small amount of blood rushed from his brain to his penis he immediately became light headed and suffered an attitude adjustment.

The war in Viet Nam was over, at least for the Yanks, the Cold War still raged on and the price of

52

booze had hit a bench mark high. An entire dollar for a beer and a dollar twenty-five for a whiskey!

Was there no god?!

There were a new slew of sitcoms out including *All in the Family* featuring the comically racist Archie Bunker and Barney Miller, probably the most realistic cop show ever dealing with day-to-day routines in a station house. Finally U.S. industry was on the rise, or so we were told.

All seemed as it should be.

Then came those pesky little Japs with their pesky affordable cars and their pesky pain-in-the-ass reasonable gas mileage engines. To top it all off the little bastards had the balls to re-engineer their cars to meet American safety standards! Along with millions of workers, like the people of Hiroshima and Nagasaki, the U.S. auto industry was about to be nuked. Pay back's a bitch.

Although Toyota had brought some cars to the States back in the late Fifties, the first signs of the actual full-on invasion appeared on most U.S. streets in the early Seventies in the form of the Mitsubishi Galant, a compact car reminiscent of a pregnant roller skate that had perhaps been raped by a Lincoln Town Car. The following forward recon units were composed mainly of other cars made by Mitsubishi, those nice people who brought you World War II.

As if that wasn't enough of an affront to American sensibility, they got upwards of forty miles to the gallon, 25-30% more efficient than the American land yachts which were quickly becoming as expensive to fill up in one go as it costs to have a kid. Only you got to keep your kid for at least 18 years. Maybe not always a good thing.

While the American sign of prestige and success was to drive through your neighborhood in a Pontiac, Caddy or Lincoln, unbeknownst to the good people of Peoria, Illinois or Flint, Michigan the measurement of success to the average working class Japanese was to have a friend who owned a car. Especially a car made by Mitsubishi.

It was about two weeks after the fantasy of *The Rocky Horror* midnight show and our Big O feast in Oakland that the real horror show began for a million steel workers in the Steel Valley stretching across Ohio, Pennsylvania and West Virginia with devastating knock-on effects for the dirt poor coal miners of several other states.

After closer examination, and at the risk of earning the undesirable label of 'communists' and being euphemistically tarred and feathered by the public, a small handful of people in the industry quietly acknowledged that, perhaps, just maybe, Japanese steel was every bit as good as American steel. Ergo the prevalent redneck argument that Japanese cars were not safe due to inferior steel was shot to shit.

The same kind of 'scientific' testing used by the big tobacco companies to prove there was no proof that tobacco hadn't yet been proven to be bad for you, had been applied to the testing of Japanese steel.

Apparently those million odd cancer patients who died every year and also just happened to be smokers, we were told, was pure coincidence.

The race to prove Japanese cars were unsafe came to a screeching halt.

As I drove along U.S. Route 80 West heading back to college that afternoon, I have to admit the DJ's and talking heads on the Three O'clock News had a point regarding the uncontrolled and cancerous spread of unemployment in the valley.

The U.S. Steel mill along Route 80 was no less than a full mile and half long and it was many a night I drove past and watched in awe as they rolled out one 50 yard long, two foot square glowing, red hot steel ingot after another to sit on the exterior rollers and cool over night in the outside air. Tool laden men scurrying around the yard in golf carts and on foot.

That night the entire U.S. Steel mill complex, to include the parking lot, looked like the set of a zombie movie.

When I got back to Youngstown the devastation hit even more emphatically home.

Next morning the tiny, downtown, two room unemployment office three blocks from my dorm was inundated by more than three thousand former steel workers lined up out the door and around the block. A scene that would be repeated through rain or shine for better than the next five to six months, day-in and day-out.

The workers were told they had been 'laid off', a cute Americanism intended to mean, "It's slow now but there will be work in the future and you'll be among the first we call back", but in reality meant, "Thanks for your loyal contribution of what were probably the best years of your life, but you are now a redundant component in our global mass market". 'And remember . . .' as the tens of thousands of bumper stickers, tee shirts and billboards which suddenly appeared across America read, 'Buy American!'

Over the ensuing months and later years all manner of solutions were sought.

The earliest efforts were protests which evolved into work stoppages by the dwindling work force still in the mills and factories as they too saw no end in sight to the rapidly advancing 'down-sizing' as the spin doctors pitched it.

Some desperately industrious groups formed their own tiny companies and attempted to negotiate a buy over on a time share basis from the mill owners but the idea was doomed from the start. There weren't enough of them to muster a fraction of the former brobdingnagian profits the steel mills reaped. The workers had no money and the banks were being bled dry as, even in the boom days, there was never really much actual cash in the vaults anyway. As in the days leading up to the Great Crash of '29, everything had been done on word of mouth, a handshake and credit.

Even the old American stand-by, the law suit was attempted, but with no money for the high powered, high priced, fast talking lawyers required to track down chase and nail the fat cat industrialists and union leaders who had succeeded in raping the entire Ohio Valley, it was like pissing off of a tall building into the wind. On a windy day with an updraft.

Above all everyone seemed to be overlooking, or were in denial of, one simple fact; American steel was no longer a viable, competitive commodity because American cars were no longer practical.

Like the Flu Epidemic of 1919, the Crash of '29 or the rise of Boy Bands nobody saw it coming, couldn't sort it out or explain it when it hit.

Eventually a compromise was reached. The Japanese would still manufacture the parts for their autos but would move their assembly plants to the U.S. and let the Americans assemble them. Under Japanese supervision of course.

The American workers weren't happy about that stipulation but I got it straight away.

I remembered the concentration the three hash slingers had displayed back on Forbes Avenue at the Big O as I watched them systematically tame the crowd to the point that even the rowdies were controlled by others in the group to allow the young guys on the other side of the counter to do their jobs.

Bottom line people wanted to eat, the cooks wanted to serve them so the place could bring in money so they could get paid and for the whole thing to work everybody had to do their part.

But the thing that struck me the hardest was what I had seen a year or so earlier while being given a tour of the GM assembly plant in Detroit by a friend who worked there. The entire 45 minute tour was punctuated with stories of how they, the workers, 'fucked' with the distributors and dealers with no consideration for the ultimate loser, the consumer.

Apparently it was great fun to deposit empty Coke bottles in the rocker panels of a car still on the assembly line before the step panel was riveted on. This caused the consumer, usually the first to discover the annoying knocking when they drove the car home, to return it to the dealer who had to pay a mechanic to find and fix the problem.

Other fun things to deposit in rocker panels were items of partially eaten food such as banana peels. This was even more thrilling because as the food began to rot it gave off an odor. These guys never considered the reputation of the company and how everyone had to do their part to make the whole thing work.

Aggravating the situation was the attitude of the workers towards their supervisors which rivaled that between the L.A. cops and the blacks of the city.

Workers on the assembly line, an unskilled labor position, were making, including health and holiday benefits, upwards of $40-$45+ per hour and were pushing for more. Minimum wage in the U.S. at the time was around $1.60. They had better benefits than any U.S. soldier, teacher or most airline pilots and many novice doctors. A clear indication of a flaw in the system.

The U.S. auto industry had gotten too fat and too lazy. Worse yet they had lost pride in who they were and the dollar sign had again reared its ugly head and come to rule everything.

But Detroit, they reasoned, was the biggest auto manufacturer in the world and therefore impregnable. Indestructible. Unsinkable.

Kind'a like *Titanic*.

It was in those days that I came to realize anyone who attends university just for the sake of a sheepskin and some didactic education is a fool. The penny dropped when I observed that the men and women of the Steel Valley, now labeled the Rust Belt, had come to believe and so had come to expect that the U.S. government had owed them a living. A foreign people were attempting to break American rice bowls and so Uncle Sam was supposed to protect them with tariffs and import quotas.

The simple fact of the matter was, the Americans had lost their competitive edge. Their ability to concentrate and focus to what was needed to get the job done and so, like a 15 year old marriage, had 'settled into' the relationship they had with their livelihoods.

Divorce was inevitable.

Regardless of what happens from the time of finishing this essentially pointless essay that may never get read beyond a few friends and family, it's been a pretty good God damned road so far and I'm God damned glad I bought my ticket and am looking forward to the rest of the ride.

See ya. I'm going to the movies.

Probably a comedy.

THE END

GOD SPELLED BACKWARDS IS DOG
(First published in October, 2011)

"I'll pray for you!" A Christian said to journalist Christopher Hitchens.

"And I'll think for you." He responded.

In line with the being aware of the times we live in, I've recently been awakened to the growing social movement away from organized religion and towards atheism. Apparently there's even a section now in bookshops. Hopefully this will at least balance the 15% of the world's one point two billion Muslims which the various security agencies around the world estimate are classified as 'radical' meaning they want to see an end to western civilization. Let me save you the math.

15% of one billion is roughly a shit load. Scary. Remember that paranoia following JFK's assassination? 9/11 kicked that up another five notches.

The Muslims' arguments against reasonable people being afraid of or against in any way the Muslim religion is that the majority of Muslims are peaceful people, that is opposed to violence.

The majority of Germans were good, peace loving people before WWII. But when the Nazis caused the slaughter of 60 million innocents the majority of Germans, who were peace loving people opposed to violence, were irrelevant.

As Stalin rampaged through the largest country in the world and disposed of 20 million, (conservative estimate), the millions of Russians who were peace loving were irrelevant.

The Chinese Communist revolution disposed of untold millions, and the peaceful majority played no part in stopping them.

When the Vatican, supported by the millions of peaceful Christians went on their little spree during the Spanish Inquisition and another million died for god, the majority were nowhere to be found.

Then there was Pol Pot and the Khmer Rouge.

The simple 'truth' is that religion is never about gods and goddesses, truth, salvation or redemption or any other bullshit along those lines. It's about what every political party before, after and since is about; money and power.

The dedicated and devout Muslims would have us all living in the 7th Century. Living in the 7th Century would be rough. No You Tube, no porn, no boy bands . . . hmmm, no boy bands? No, no, never mind at least gotta have my porn. You ever seen a Botticelli painting? Those chicks were no strangers to a lasagna dinner, a bit chunky know-what-I-mean? Not my idea of quality porn.

Bottom line is the peaceful majority of Muslims are a little too quiet for most Westerners myself included.

Curious thing about gods, particularly the ones of monotheistic origins. They are a deity who has chosen to have a special relationship with only one of the millions of species on earth on one of the billons of worlds in the universe and for some inexplicable reason have an intense if not perverse interest in what we do in the dark when we're naked.

I'm not too sure how you base an entire civilization on those features as a moral code. But it was done.

Any logical person must question a god who tells us by law, (written in stone mind you), that we are not supposed to kill each other but who wipes entire swaths of populations from the earth with bad weather and temperamental geological structures because they have somehow displeased him.

Not very good at leading by example is he, (She?).

If god is a woman at least that would explain why the moon rotates in 28 day cycles and people go crazy once a month.

A former girlfriend once fended off an entire SWAT platoon for six hours one time when aunt flow was visiting. The day after, when things calmed down the Chief of Police phoned up to see if she was available to help train other SWAT Team negotiators.

It's hard to tell a man's religion by just looking at him, making religious recognition difficult.

Jews don't recognize Jesus as the Messiah, Protestants don't recognize The Pope as the head of the church, none of the Judeo-Christian religions recognize the Hindus who in turn don't recognize them, and when they take off their white shirts and black ties, Jehovah's Witnesses' don't recognize each other in porno shops.

For the educated the non-existence of an omnipotent entity with his finger on the pulse of the universe to the point that he knows how many hairs are on your head is a far gone conclusion, but the real question is, how far can we hope this reverse magnetism of pro-enlightenment and anti-organized religion will go?

Pretty far we hope.

I have been asked by numerous religious people why I don't believe in their gods? I ask them if they believe in others' gods. They inevitably say no. Well that's the same reason I don't believe in your god.

The fact that I've been told that some of my writings about gods is offensive, is to me, quite frankly, offensive.

Aside from the peaceful majority of Muslims not appearing to take much of a stand against their psychotically violent 'brothers' is the lunacy of political correctness which too has run its course.

It's time rational people pointed out that there are stupid people out there and for no other reasons then for those of humanity they need to be informed that they are stupid. They must be told because, unfortunately, you can't fix stupid.

Well, you can but it hurts.

What about other religions? Religions other than the one true religion . . . oh wait! That's all of them.

I mean other religions besides Islam.

The Christians have clearly seen their time. Between their endless fractionalization into numerous sects, the sexual scandals which have finally surfaced after hundreds of years and the financial challenges which have arisen due to the fact that honest hard working people are no longer required by law to support those freeloaders through tithes, their days as an influential entity in the civilized world are numbered.

The Jews played the right card from the time before Moses when they kicked off basing their cultural integrity as a people on money. Finances. Being persecuted all the time means you can never really have any roots anywhere which means you have to keep your assets as liquid as possible, which means money.

Let's not forget that they were persecuted largely because they didn't recognize everybody else's' gods.

My theory is that the reason Pharaoh chased them all across that foreboding, bone roasting desert was probably because he was pissed off that they took all their golden idols with them. In one week the Egyptian GNP was halved and tourists stopped visiting the pyramids. The Great Pyramids at Giza don't look all old and beat-up due to their age, they always looked that way, from the time the Jews left and they fell into disarray due to cutbacks. All the menial labor jobs had to be filled by Egyptians themselves.

Pharaoh's popularity probably plummeted.

All jokes aside, Buddhists aren't really religious in the way we understand religion, that is a belief system governed by a Christian-Judeo like dogma. Buddhism is a philosophy. But they'll probably be at least one of those little guys left in his flimsy, yellow robe putting incense on the smoldering ash heap after the first nuclear war.

I read where reincarnation is making a comeback. Unless they have a falling out. In which case I wonder could we still call it 'having a beef'? You know, because they're vegetarians?

Personally, after spending so much time observing American politics, particularly this latest crop of Democrats, I think there might be something to the reincarnation argument. Hard to believe you could get that many that fucked up in one lifetime.

But what about the real nutters? The Jehovah's Witnesses, Hare Krisnas and Mormons? *Watchtower Magazine*, drums, clogging up airports begging for donations for large colorful books and polygamy?

Maybe if someone comes up with a plan to herd them altogether we might luck out and, like women's menstrual cycles in a women's dorm, the Rapture, Armageddon and the Great Reckoning will all synchronize and wipe them out.

So, someday when religion has become a thing people are forced to do for community service to humor the remnants of 'The Believers', to keep them from committing suicide and costing the taxpayers extra fees for emergency services and burial costs, Jehovah's Witnesses, Hare Krishna and Mormons will one day merge and be given a chunk of land in the deserts of East Texas where they won't be able to bother honest people because they'll be too busy knocking on each other's doors while banging each other's drums and babbling about the end.

Which raises another important question; once they eventually merge will they all have to shave their heads and wear those orange bath towels? And if so, where will they put those black bondage strips everyone thinks are retro, 1960's, ties?

THE END

THE LAST TIME WE DREAMT
(First published in June, 2012)

"When you become literate in science you empower yourself to know when someone is bullshitting you." - Dr. Neil Degrasse Tyson, Director Hayden Planetarium, Museum of Natural History N.Y.C., New York

There can be no debate over the fact that as humans we are meant to roam, wander and explore. Ever since *Homo habilus* poked his head out of the relative safety of the Olduvai Gorge in East Africa two million years ago and moseyed on over to the Laetoli plains asking, "I wonder what's over **that** hill?", little kids have been poking their heads in kitchen cabinets and old retirees have been pulling up stakes from Jesus-Christ-Its-Cold, Minnesota and moving to Fort Lauderdale, Florida.

A couple of million years later, after the Laetoli plains with the launch of a two foot diameter steel ball called Sputnik, humans had space programs.

And a space race.

We'll never know exactly what motivated the first Homo to embark upon his voyage of discovery. Maybe local resources were getting low, maybe there were some nasty beasties who were getting a little too successful at hunting for people flesh or maybe the first guy to set out on the journey wasn't such a wise monkey and got himself caught monkeying around with another monkey's monkey.

Which would account for that big dent in the first scull Louis and Mary Leakey found down in the Olduvai Gorge.

But what we have learned from all this travelling, shifting and moving around is that human existence is largely about hope. Hope for the future. Hope for something better.

Hope that some of the people who show up at your house once a year on Thanksgiving and Christmas aren't really related to you by blood and that maybe they just stopped to ask directions and your elderly aunt invited them in.

Organized religion, as well as all the other political parties, have developed ways to exploit this hope thing from day one and have cleverly been able to capitalize on it. For possibly as long as the last forty thousand years they have managed to corner the market on the sale of hope and have successfully transformed it into a quite lucrative business.

"Come to our church, pray with us, read our book, hold us in high accord and we'll give you hope!" Spelled S-A-L-V-A-T-I-O-N.

For a small fee.

"Put us in office, give us power and privilege, give us guys with guns and badges but make us exempt from your laws and we'll give you hope!" Spelled R-E-P-R-E-S-E-N-T-A-T-I-O-N.

For your votes.

How can I make such blasphemous statements? Easy. What's the antonym for scientist? Well, it's logical when you think about it, there are several. Priest, politician, mullah, rabbi. Pick one, these are all equal opportunity exploiters.

The scientist has the good of mankind at heart. The politician has the good of himself at heart.

The 'servants' of God, priests, rabbis, mullahs and ministers, are on the fence. They preach the good of God for the good of mankind, with a small gratuity for themselves.

Don't forget to tip your servers. Gratuity automatically included for groups over ten.

"Oh, but there are good politicians!"

Possibly, just like until 1938 it was believed that the coelacanths were extinct. Then a young fisherman off the coast of South Africa caught one. One.

I have no faith that honest politicians are a Lazarus taxon, but as one of my old commanders, who was physically incapable of making a decision, used to say, "You never know!"

***

Our circa 1870's granite and brick school building was made with walls so thick and tall that most speculate it was a converted 13th Century Norman castle minus the moat. It was sturdy but not roomy. It was so sturdy in fact that it had been designated a bomb shelter in case of nuclear attack.

As all the well-groomed, uniformed primary students from several classes, 35-40 per class, shuffle through the long narrow halls around the stacks of emergency food rations and olive, drab green, three foot high metal canisters marked "Drinking Water" we were gently shepherded into the back of our classroom. It was the late 1960's.

The thirty days emergency food and water rations for 100 were compliments of the newly created Civil Defense branch of the government.

They mysteriously appeared in all the local schools one weekend shortly after the Russians launched their first successful manned capsule. Far from the reassuring asset the military envisioned they would be, the big green cans of food and water with the big yellow 'C.D.' logo only ratcheted up the tension of the world situation. Not least of which because there are over 500 people in the school. If the shit hits the fan, and there is a nuclear war, looks like 400 people are going on a diet!

Also, suspicions were growing that the Soviets were up to no good down in that little island south of Florida called Cuba.

The later months, essentially the last quarters of the years of the early Sixties, never seemed to go very well for politics and the politicians.

During the first week in December of '61, as massive racial violence continued to tear across the country, the U.S. decade long involvement in Viet Nam was sealed when JFK sent the first contingent of 'unofficial' troops to Saigon.

Then in October 1962 JFK came on television and told us about the Cuban Missile Crisis and let us all know, in very eloquent language, that within the next week there was a chance the world might be incinerated.

We weren't worried though, we had our thirty days rations and our 3/4 inch wooden desks to hide under.

On November the 22nd the following year, a triple disaster for the country, JFK was assassinated, LBJ inherited the reins of power and *The Warren Commission* was commissioned to hide the facts of who commissioned whom to assassinate JFK.

While the U.S. was compelled to buy back from Cuba the last eleven hundred guys who were captured during the disastrous Bay of Pigs invasion for $53 million in food parcels, on October 12th the infamous *Columbus Day Storm* hit with 300km/h winds killing dozens and wreaking hundreds of millions in damage.

It used to be said that if a young politician was going to make his bones in U.S. politics it would probably be during the last calendar quarter of the year.

If all that weren't enough, just when we thought things were settling down, the day after Christmas one of the worst recorded disasters in United States history occurred. Like a genocidal tsunami from the gods, Beatlemania hit the country.

The total number of teenaged, female minds lost is still unknown.

Back in the school no one knew what was going on but we blindly obeyed the penguins directing the boys to move and stack the heavy oaken desks to the side as the girls restowed all the book bags in the walk-through cloak room behind the front blackboard to make more room in the class.

It's Tuesday around two in the afternoon, almost time for the three o'clock bell and to get out of school, but the urgency of the frenzy had

71

everyone distracted.

With everyone sitting tightly packed, all across the floor, (kind'a like in all the news footage we were fed about the overcrowded schools in South East Asia), two kids from an upper grades wheeled in a tall trolley holding the school's 32" Magnavox, 12 channel, color television set.

Now we know something's definitely up!

Being a Catholic school St. Aloysius Primary had a television. The kids over at P.S. #39, (Public School 39, which meant government funded), also had a television, but they had to go home to watch it.

Once the three classes were packed in, settled in and tuned in our teacher quieted us down and the Principal, Sister Mary Knuckle Thump, squeezed her six foot two inch, 300 pound frame through the front door and lumbered to the front of the room.

As she peered down, (we always assumed it was a she because they called her 'sister'), we maintained silence to the point of holding our breath. I think one kid in the back was so nervous he wet his pants.

She announced we were going to watch the United States Navy recover the space capsule of Astronaut Lt. Col. John Glenn, the first American to orbit the earth.

None of us had ever heard of a 'capsule' except of course when dad had a headache or when he had to run to the pharmacy to get some for mom. But that was only once a month when some relative named aunt Flo would show up.

Funny we never got to meet Aunt Flo at

Thanksgiving dinner.

The lights dimmed, the telly crackled to life and in blurred reds, yellows and blues, Walter Cronkite, the man who could tell America the Martians had just landed in New Jersey and they would believe him, sparked onto the screen.

He sat at his desk in the CBS studio with a diorama of the Mercury capsule pretend circling a mini-earth taped to the wall behind him. He held a sheaf of papers he never referred to and spoke to camera.

We have just received word that the space craft has been sighted on radar.

For the next several minutes Walter took us inside the *Friendship Seven* space capsule via radio waves, (no video), as they played the conversation between Glenn and somebody on the other end of the phone named 'Steelhead'.

The capsule, for that's what it's called, a 'capsule', will descend by parachute to predetermined coordinates in the middle of the Atlantic . . .

Walter informed us.

We had been told all of our young lives that AT&T could do anything so we collectively wondered how long that telephone wire must have been to reach from the CBS studios up into that tiny space capsule and moreover, why it wouldn't get tangled up during orbit?

73

Walter droned on.

We patiently waited for footage of the 'capsule' while the garbled radio chatter with Steelhead continued.

The bell rang. No one moved, just looked around. Staring down at us from the front corner of the dimly lit room, arms crossed over a chest large enough to feed Zimbabwe, the head penguin pursed her razor thin lips signaling, "Don't even think about moving" her stern look conveyed. We didn't move.

Walter cranked on.

We take you now live to the deck of the U.S.S. Noa where . . .

A camera picked up a long shot of a Sea King helicopter hovering near the bobbing Mercury capsule. The side door of the copter opened and three guys in black rubber suits, swim fins and masks jumped out. From all the way up in that unbelievably cooler that cool helicopter. Jumped. Into the middle of the ocean! Into the waves in the middle of the Atlantic Ocean! Then the three man-fish, as if born of dolphins, these three crazy guys swam for the dancing capsule which looked like it was being eaten alive by the sea itself.

The helo edged closer to the action and dropped a big orange thing into the water. The swimmers retrieved it and started wrapping it around the capsule.

From where I sat looking up at that 32" color Magnavox with the 12 channels, watching the recovery operation, for that's what it was called a recovery operation, I was struck by how cool it was. Cool enough to freeze the Arctic! So cool it belonged in the Arctic. On Pluto!

Although I had no idea what they were called, I knew that I wanted to be one of those swimmer guys who jumped out of helicopters and airplanes and did neat shit.

At that exact moment I knew that I wanted to be a Navy frogman.

It was an early epiphany and although I didn't realize it at the time, those unnamed guys jumping out of that helicopter into the Atlantic, changed my perspective of my future forever. They gave me something to shoot for. To dream about.

They gave me inspiration which bred hope.

***

In a little under five hours Glenn had been blown into space by a quarter of a million gallons of rocket fuel, streaked through three earth days and three nights and parachuted safely into the vast Atlantic Ocean within 400 meters of his target area.

And from there the Mercury missions continued. Then followed the Gemini launches paving the way for the long awaited and promised Apollo missions. The ones that would finally free mankind from the constraints of earth and being relegated to a single-planet species.

In July of 1969 man walked on the moon. But also in July of 1969 the war in Viet Nam was escalating. Of course, in the politicians' defense, war has always proven to be a sure money maker,

75

extremely profitable providing you can drag it out long enough. In contrast, the space program only **took** money and all it gave in return was information. Information that would one day provide real alternatives to the survival of the human race. However the one man who was intelligent enough to convert scientific advances into votes, JFK, was dead.

So suddenly a government ridden with the cancer of corruption confronting an inevitable loss to the communists in Viet Nam, declared the space dream was over. And in the space of one to two years all those things that should have been, could have been, were no longer not only declared impossible, but erased from the drawing boards and imaginations of the scientists as well as the people.

Unfortunately the price we, the primary school students of America, had to pay due to special interests such as GM, McDonald Douglas and other industries backed by a plethora of auxiliary industries, was that the Washedupton brain trust calculated, (probably with an abacus), that everyone from age five to fifteen must take and excel at math.

Suddenly we needed a whole generation of physicists, mathematicians and astrophysicists to 'catch up' with the Russians. The same Russians who were starving in the streets because their government was spending all their tax money on catching up with the Americans in the Space Race.

Ironic given that the Russians were force feeding their youth math and physics and steering them away from disciplines of their own choice and now here was America following suit.

Fortunately the Ruskies didn't jump off a bridge.

Years later after July 1969, no one thought to ask: What about all those budding mathematicians, physicists, astrophysicists and astronomers that were created by forcing everyone to take algebra and calculus in primary school?

America lost two full generations of artists, songwriters, poets, painters, sculptures, dancers, historians and other would-be humanitarians while the space program stagnated.

LBJ to Obama, a total of 48 years, half a century, in which save for some satellites, important satellites but satellites none the less, and a space station half built by the Russians, (Remember those guys?), which had already been half designed by the time Kennedy was assassinated, the only thing that came out of NASA, that was **allowed** to come out of NASA due to restricted funding, were the projects that benefited big industry.

From the late Fifties to the late Sixties, when America got serious about space travel, less than a generation had passed. Neil Armstrong achieved the goal set less than a decade before.

Half a century, compared to a decade and a half. Something was wrong.

An age-old argument has it that America is wasting money on space at the expense of programs on earth.

When you consider that, according to Dr. Neil Tyson, the entire cost of Mars mission of 2015 was about the same cost as one day in Afghanistan, that's a hard argument to sustain.

Given the inflated enemy of the Mid-East, which unfortunately will never ever go away, and all the cash the U.S. has dumped into fighting it, we not only could have established a station on The Sea of Tranquility but could have established a pretty good foothold towards colonizing and terra-forming Mars.

With all the shit that was happening back on earth in the Sixties, race riots, Nixon, police brutality, Nixon, government scandals, Nixon and industrially induced poverty, the hope of a better future, fostered by a progressive, sustainable space program, was a pretty damned big deal. There was hardly a day when the folks on the street didn't talk about what was happening with NASA. Always with a taint of hope for the future.

One Saturday morning my father borrowed the train fare to buy a couple of tokens and take me Uptown to the Allied Chemical Building in Times Square where there was a full scale 50:1 layout of NASA's first proposed moon base on the Sea Of Tranquility on exhibit.

Standing on tiptoes to peer through the top of the glass of the exhibit I remember thinking: *This is not a cheesy Hollywood movie set. This is the real shit! And when these guys travel back and forth from the moon twenty years in the future, I'm gonna be one of those guys who jumps out of the helicopter into the water to help pluck them from the ocean!*

I remember this well because it was also the time we saw the first one inch and a half square wrist TV being demonstrated upstairs in Macy's on 34th Street.

It wasn't till years later that I learned from my mother that my father walked the eleven miles, one way, from Lower Manhattan out to Flushing Meadows in Queens, (because he had to save the $2 for admission), to visit the 1964 New York World's Fair a few years earlier.

I later got why. Hope. Hope that there was some kind of future in store for him and his family. Something beyond the relentless daily physical and mental grind of his part-time stevedore's job across the Hudson River in Jersey City.

I realize now, as I'm writing this, that maybe that Allied Chemical exhibit wasn't just for me.

I consider myself ridiculously lucky to have been born in a time when I could live through the breaking of the sound barrier, men descending in the bathysphere and the bathyscaph, the invention of the rocket, space launches, construction of the International Space Station, walking on the moon, and the onset of the Mars One mission. I won't be around when we colonize or terra-form Mars but knowing it's gonna happen in my kids' lifetime makes me a little less apprehensive about buying the farm because it puts the big picture in a tangible perspective.

It took the Soviet and American governments fifty years to figure out the answer to the question we were all asking back in the fourth grade: 'Why ain't we working together?"

Personal motivation, the greed of politics and world domination were concepts we had not yet been introduced to as children when we pondered that question.

The poor judgment, dishonesty and greed exhibited by the present day, virtually stagnant congress which has now evolved into part and parcel of our everyday life, is inexcusable. As they play political party Parcheesi for the next fiscal quarter and they vie for the next election, planning their own futures they have clearly forgotten, or willfully ignored, that they have received the torch from the Congress in the time of the scientific Sixties. They have mortgaged the countries' future for political gains and war profits stripping the next 3 to 4 generations of hope for the future, and they must now be forced to see the light.

Now is the time for the ladies and gentlemen of the esteemed Congress to make amends and reinstitute the all but abandoned space program, not to its former glory, but to its future, further glory.

They must do this, if for no other reason than to reinstitute hope in the future for Americans and convince them that, despite slipping to 14th in Education and 44th in Health Care, according to a 2015 Bloomberg L.P. report, leaving only 33% of Americans happy with the way things are going in their country, they can maybe one day again hold their heads up and think as one rather than a rabble of special interest groups pointing the finger at each other like a bunch of school boys caught in a stolen car.

Yesterday we had the Cold War, The Iron Curtain and the Space Race. Today we have technology and understanding at its highest level since we abandoned and moved on from the Olduvai Gorge.

Science, as opposed to religion, offers more than hope. It offers tangible results which is why it is the more potent weapon of hope.

If, as John Dewey espoused, ". . . politics is the shadow of business cast over society", then it's time we stepped back into the light.

ASSESSING CLIMATE CHANGE

THE END

There's An App for That Two!
is Dedicated to:

Dr. George Kelly, Ph.D. Senior U.N. researcher in
Communicable Diseases, former Chair of Biology
at YSU and U.S. Army Medic who landed at
Normandy and marched across Europe in Patton's
Third Army in a time when gaping wounds were
sprinkled with sulphur powder and closed over with
safety pins.
He's seen some shit.

Thank You George.

INTRODUCTION TO APP TWO

Awareness of who, what, where, and most importantly why, we are is now and always has been the driving force behind human existence.

In the following pages politics, religion and science will be discussed at various levels and opinions with which you may or may not agree. It is also possible that some of this may help you form, or at least solidify, some of your own opinions on these topics.

While science strives to shed ever more light on the answers to these questions, who? what? where? and why? the ages old religious establishments, which have successfully leached onto and woven themselves into the political fabric of every nation on earth and therefore wield a disproportionate force of power then they have rightfully earned, strive to stop or turn back the clock and frustrate the gains of honest men.

Trailing behind mankind as a whole, organized religion has made a limited contribution to the advancement of humankind but has now outlived its usefulness and must be allowed to slowly wither on the offshoots of the vines of civilization. If we are to keep advancing we must do so on the precepts of reason and empirical knowledge shedding the clouds of superstition which have obscured the quest for truth as evidenced by fact.

Most people agree that there are two things that you shouldn't discuss in mixed company and polite settings, religion and politics. There is a reason you have never heard anyone say; "Now when we get to the Henderson's George, don't bring up science!" It's always don't bring up religion or politics. Which I normally did . . . which is probably why I'm not still married, but let's not open up that old wound! The point is nobody ever says 'don't bring up science' because science is not controversial. It is either a fact or it is yet to be proven or disproved. However, and more importantly, it is not brought up because most people are not science literate.

If you've never heard this said about politics and religion, then you're probably too young to appreciate these essays. For those of you who fit this category think about the politics and religion thing as Super Nintendo versus XBox only on steroids and where seven billion plus lives are involved. No pressure mind you.

The question that then arises is, given we need 'leaders' and, both our political and religious leaders have continually lied, misled and betrayed us who do we 'trust' in so far as the word trust still retains any semblance of its traditional meaning?

Well until they attempt to become politicians or religious fanatics, we trust the scientists and educators. Not the political organizations with a powerful political lobby; any of them may represent or, who are founded on political goals or purport to gather huge fortunes for 'research' in areas such as cancer. And certainly not the science people who work for the big pharmaceuticals who are in it for the big bucks.

I'm talking about the guys whose primary goal

in life is the search for knowledge, the people commonly referred to as the 'pure' scientists. The people in the trenches. The guys who get up in the morning and show up at the labs, the remote research sites or the classrooms and work through the day and many times into and through the night to fight to get one step closer to obtain new data based on work which others did before them. Data that some other scientist can apply, use and find to discover one more thing that will bring us closer to the facts and one step further from the myths, monsters and magical beings people have 'believed' in for far too long.

And remember, while the suffix -ology denotes the scientific study of a given subject, prefixing it with 'scient' doesn't make it scientific. Or real for that matter.

The other topic in this handful of stories and essays, besides science and religion, is the other forbidden subject, politics.

Abuse of the English lexicon, largely by those in politics, has led to a significant chunk of our language being reduced to a hollow, meaningless vocabulary. Words such as equal, solemn promise and dedication when used nowadays, particularly by the political elite, answer the question, "How do you know when a politician is lying?"

His mouth is moving.

The obvious counter argument is of course that old chestnut, "But there are some good politicians!"

Unarguably. There are, probably. Somewhere. Just because I never met one doesn't mean they ain't there. But bottom line is, the good ones don't outweigh the bad ones and don't appear to be putting up much of a front against the bad ones.

These writings are intended to be observational in nature with some opinion thrown in for flavor. Okay, a lot of opinion. Opinion with which you may or may not agree. If you agree, thank you, if not; write your own collection.

Thank you for taking the time to have a look at this and I hope you enjoy the read. Feel free to respond with your own feedback on one of my sites.

P. Kelly

READERS
(First published in June, 2012)

The bed-ridden old man made no attempt to mask his strong sense of indignation as he spoke.

"You **have** to do it, you know you do!" He demanded.

"What'ch you talkin' 'bout, '**have** to do it'? I only got's to do two things! Grow old and dies!" Without allowing the old man's verbal assault to interrupt her sheet folding duties the middle-aged Grenadian nurse snapped back.

"What about pay taxes?" He snidely countered which caused her to pause contemplatively.

Ernie Greenbaum, a victim of the Big C who was given six months to live, had occupied bed number five of the clinic's two patient room in the retirement home's delightfully decorated medical ward, for the last year and half.

Hunt's Point Nursing Home is a respectable geriatric storage facility where middle aged YUPPIE's deposit their elderly parents to quietly await their expiration date. Particularly when said parents become too much of an imposition on their busy lives.

The quaint but antiquated European and Asian practice of extended families, all living under the same roof, makes no sense. Children looking after their parents is after all, counter intuitive. Common knowledge dictates that it's meant to be the other way round.

Hunt's Point is also a conducive arrangement while one waits out the days, months, or God forbid, years, for one's inheritance to come to fruition.

Respectable, the key phrase utilized by the H.P.N.H. sales and P.R. staff, of course means expensive. After all how could you face your friends, family and rabbi if you didn't give your folks the best care available in their last days on earth? And where else could you expect the best medical care available if not at the most respectable, most expensive commercial facility?

"Okay, you're *supposed* to do it." Ernie relented but continued to press the attack. "You are a nurse aren't you? I mean you did attend some kind of nursing school at some point in time?" He adjusted himself on the bed and jutted his head forward in challenge. "Just a shot in the dark here."

Wilhemina shifted to one leg and put both hands on her hips as she replied.

"I have you know Mr. Greenbaum that I be a proud graduate of *The Holy Immaculate Heart of Mary Trinidad School of Nursin'* man!"

He focused at the dancing clown just over her shoulder on the wall behind her. In order to make them more respectable all the rooms were themed. Ernie's room, 2B, was the 'Happy' room. Upon arrival they put him in 2C but nobody saw the dark irony until Ernie's M.D. pointed it out.

"Well then you must have at one time or another at least accidentally touched a psychology book which had a chapter on geriatric psychology at some point in both your months at the HIM school of nursing?" Wilhemina Donahee remained unimpressed. "You know, the part that teaches you about an elderly person's need to maintain some semblance of a sense of productivity? Self-reliance, self-worth?" He iterated.

"You keep givin' me so much of you guff and I gonna give you self sumthin' that's worth it! And a nutter thing, how you know so much 'bout geriatric psychology?!"

"Because I am heavily involved with anti-social media." She cocked her head and stared. "Books!" He said as he brandished his hard back copy of *Cyrano de Bergerac*. "I read." He answered with no attempt to hide his annoyance. She again assumed the expression of a cat just been shown a card trick and glared at the volumes stacked up behind him on the head board, several of which had spilled over onto the floor. "Yes, books. That's right, I'm one of **those** people! Like the mysteries of the Bermuda Triangle, Emilia Earhart and Jimmy Hoffa. Like the lost city of Atlantis. A reader!"

"ATLANTIS, OHH!" He felt a small measure of relief as his words appeared to have struck a chord in her. "I loves that place!" She declared as he looked at her with ever evolving perplexity. "Me and my sister goes there every Summer!"

She wheeled the chrome medicine cart over to his bedside and handed him two small plastic cups with several tablets in each. She then leaned in and, taking him into her confidence, switched to a loud whisper. "Last year she won 275 dallas on the crappy tables!"

He looked up from the bed and stared.

"I don't suppose either one of you thought to buy a book with the money?"

"We was gonna, but they was no more money left after we bought ourselves them nice shoes!" She giggled.

"Shoes?!"

"You know, them things you wear on your feets?" He exuded a deep breath. "Speakin' a wearin' stuff, times wearin' out for yourself!"

"Yeah, I got cancer! Thanks for the update!"

"I mean when you gonna finish writin' dat last will you been sittin' on since you come here?" He fought back a string of profanities. "Just cause you ain't signed no will papers don't mean deaf gonna wait for you! Deaf don't wait for nobody!"

"So with a double negative does that means death **does** wait for some people?"

"I'm talkin' 'bout we needs to know how you want yo' remains treated. You don't put it in writin', they just gonna cremate your old white behind." She chastised as she passed him two more med cups with capsules in them.

"No cremation!" He barked.

"Why not? Ain't nuthin' to be afraid of! You ain't gonna feel nuffin'!"

"Why waste all my elements?" He argued.

"Elements?!"

"The elements I have been exchanging with the earth all these years in the most perfect example of symbiosis imaginable?"

"Sympathy for what?"

"Sym-bi-o-. . . never mind."

"Even a hard ass'd man like yo'self must be

thinkin' about what happens after your deaf, man!"

"No, no I don't. I do think about what happens if I go deaf. And I also sometimes think about what happens after my death. My kids bury me, they feel guilty long enough to extract a moderate amount of sympathy from their friends and significant others for a short period, they attend the reading of my will then they all meet again in court in 30 days to dispute the will and fight over my estate." He adjusted himself higher up on the bed.

"I'm talking 'bout where **you** goes after you dies!" She insisted.

"By being buried without a coffin my natural elements, the things of which I am made, the things which came from the stars themselves to create me, create all of us, can return to mother earth more quickly and efficiently and are there to be shared by the other inhabitants of this planet. And who knows? Possibly at some later date by inhabitants of another, more distant, hopefully more advanced planet!"

She passed him his last two medicine cups.

"I'm talkin' bout death man! What's you talkin' 'bout?! Space mans, aliens and green monsters?! I means ain't you worried 'bout deaf? What happens after youse dead?!" Wilhemina Donahee clarified.

"Death? You want to know what I believe about death?"

"Yes! What about the good Lord, heaven and hell?!" At the word 'hell' she made the sign of the cross. "In short, what's you gonna say to Saint Peter when you gets to the Pearly Gates?"

"Miss Donahee, I am not so arrogant as to think

that my life is so important that an all knowing master of the universe, Iron Age war god though he be, is going to take time out from his busy work schedule of managing all the billions of souls on the earth to have a chat and greet me and serve tea with biscuits when I die. My life is not that important or complicated."

"You tryin' ta say you don't believe in no god?"

With a physical display of exasperation he lay down his book, folded his hands on his lap and spoke.

"The logic of belief in a supreme being, in the face of a complete and total absence of any proof, controlling everything in the known universe, but who is singularly concerned with one species of primate and who is particularly concerned with what we do in the dark, especially when we are naked, defies explanation."

"Huh!" She grunted. "That don't answer my question 'bout deaf!"

"In short, when I am, death is not. When death is, I am not."

Nurse Donahee stared back and shook her head as she gathered the inexpensive little plastic med cups which held Ernie's every expensive medicine

He chuckled as he considered the irony of the meds given him to instill hope in the face of a hopeless situation and at the expensive cost of the pretty little pills to drive away the horrible disease which he got for free, compliments of the R. J. Reynolds Tobacco Company, in faraway Raleigh Durham, North Carolina.

Of course if the pills worked, he'd still die, but on the up side Pfizer Pharmaceuticals Inc. would be able to market them for 300% of what it cost to produce them thus significantly boosting their annual bottom line. Which in turn would make their stockholders very happy. Particularly the big corporate stockholders and investors like the R. J. Reynolds Tobacco Company.

It was a circle of life kind'a thing.

THE END

WHEELCHAIRS OF THE GODS

or
Eric the Red (faced)
(First published in June, 2014)

"That writing as careless as von Däniken's, whose principal thesis is that our ancestors were dummies, should be so popular is a sober commentary on the credulousness and despair of our times. I also hope for the continuing popularity of books like *Chariots of the Gods?* in high school and college logic courses, as object lessons in sloppy thinking. I know of no recent books so riddled with logical and factual errors as the works of von Däniken."

Dr. Carl Sagan, from the foreword to *The Space Gods Revealed*

Michael Shermer, editor of *Skeptic Magazine* was featured on the TED Talks series where he gave a guest presentation on his 1997 book *Why People Believe in Weird Things*. The publication and the book focus on debunking bad, sloppy or just bullshit science.

After watching Shermer's presentation the rusty vaults of my memory creaked open and this crept out.

***

The university auditorium was packed past standing room and the overflow made a mockery of the fire codes. The flooding over into the adjoining hallways rivaled anything that happened in the New Orleans floods, not counting the apathy of George W. as he continued his golf game while dozens died, thousands scrambled for their lives and yet more millions of taxpayer's cash was flushed down the toilet because the head of FEMA, A George W. appointee, whose primary qualification for the position of helping tens of thousands in dire need of food, water and shelter was as a horse show organizer.

Every chair of all the science departments, A&P, Chemistry, Zoology, and especially Astronomy, grad students, the local Press and the few members of the general public who could squeeze in or hang from the chandeliers or rafters was in attendance.

The self-styled, self-appointed pop-cult figure, Eric von Däniken had come to speak.

Eric von Däniken was a writer who back in the late-Sixties, 1968 to be exact, wrote a best seller *Chariots of the Gods?* He was able to follow it up with several successful sequels, nineteen in fact, with all but a few featuring the word 'god'.

I guess if you're on to a money maker no sense in monkeying with the recipe.

After being completely disgraced in the public media, in 1982 he embarked on a revival tour. One of his stops was Youngstown State University in Ohio where I was on layover pursuing a degree in Zoology until I could get my ass back in the military and qualify for a slot in Special Operations.

The books, each one based on the previous edition, claimed absolute proof that technology had been given to man by visitors from other planets. In other words we're a pretty stupid bunch, and if not by the grace of some benevolent aliens from *Planet Ten*, who as far as I can figure from Däniken's writings were lost and looking for a nuclear gas station, just dropped in for directions and decided they'd teach mankind about tools. No proof of which has ever been forthcoming. But if not for these reps from the Intergalactic Red Cross we'd still be living in caves, with cloths wrapped around our heads for warmth, praying to Iron Aged war gods, killing each other and . . . Oh wait . . .

On the other hand, after seeing how many people lined up to buy his 'books', I was nearly convinced he was right about Man being too stupid to build the pyramids.

Curious no one ever made this correlation but worse yet was the rapidity with which his lunacy spread across the land.

Between claims of us being too stupid to have engineered the great architectural works of the world ourselves, having to depend on seemingly altruistic aliens and the mind muddled masses lining up to buy his books, which only reinforced his theory, I was confused.

Oh sweet irony of youth.

But then again, as his net worth is posted on line, ($30 million), I know for a fact he laughed all the way to the bank.

This event and E.v.D.'s initial success it must

be noted, was on the tail of the latest slew of reported UFO sightings following those of the Fifties and Sixties which prompted the U.S. Air Force to commission *Project Bluebook*, an 18 year detailed investigation by Capt. Donald E. Kehoe and others of all the reported U.F.O.'s which had come across the U.S.A.F.'s desks, twelve and a half thousand in all. More than a few of these reports by some very reputable people.

By the early Seventies Carl Sagan was coming to prominence, the Mercury and Gemini programs had been completed, and the Apollo missions were on schedule to continue their moon missions. Finally, it seemed, America was on the road to becoming a scientifically literate people.

However, America is a big place and no matter how much intelligent scientific proof you have, there's always going to be a minority who labor under the delusion that science is a belief system.

Largely on the weak and worn counter argument that no one could prove that technology wasn't given to mankind by aliens, Eric V.D. had spread. Echoes of the ages old 'god argument' known in educated circles as the God-of-the-gaps argument, lingered. If science can't prove it then it must mean that God did it, now resurfaced in the writings of a failed Swiss Restaurant Service Industry student.

Being completely bankrupt of the capacity for original thought and having virtually no traces of a scientific education, (Eric failed out of high school), E.v.D. thought it prudent to steal an idea from a real scientist - Dr. Carl Sagan himself. After all, if you're going to steal might as well steal from the best. Just ask John Lennon, Ray Parker Jr. and Quentin Tarantino. (See essay on originality, entitled; *On Originality*. How's that for being original?)

My scientific view of the universe set in before puberty and so was well known by anyone who knew me. Consequently gags like registering my name to sign up for Scientology meetings was a great thrill for my so-called 'friends'. As a joke, with prompting by these 'friends', my girlfriend bought me a copy of *Chariots* for my birthday.

Unaware of the initial press, (no Facebook, Twitter or You Tube in those days, just the Boob Tube and the Six O'clock News), I was under the impression that it was a serious work. Until I got through the first two pages. I really couldn't get angry at her for the joke. It was a good one. Besides, what was I going to do? The sex was too good.

This was the time I also became aware of the fact that the public, the American public anyway, will pretty much buy anything you want to sell them providing the promotional fortitude is there. Hence reality T.V., *Dr. Phil*, *Judge Judy* and late night info-mercials which is the kind of shit that evolves when people have everything they need. The days of the traveling snake oil salesmen are far from over. Just ask Nancy Pelosi.

To be fair, Eric quoted some pretty impressive sources in his book. A NASA astronaut, (John Glenn no less), the eminent anthropologist, Thor Heyerdahl of *Kon Tiki* fame and a shopping list of others with legitimate credentials.

He detailed several arguments that the general public, having little or no science education, would easily buy into. Things were improving on the education front in The States, but let's face facts, it was still The States. 24th in literacy as I type this according to UNESCO.

I shelved the 'book', something wouldn't let me toss it, and I went on with life.

A few years later in 1978 my all-time favorite science show, the only full time regular show devoted to science in American at the time, *NOVA*, featured a program, *The Case of the Ancient Astronauts*. A *TV Guide* synopsis told me it would be focused on E.v.D. himself.

It was a Sunday night, I had had a good day at the gym followed by a good meal and was getting good grades at uni. That month. In short life was good. Then the show started. Life was about to get better.

The intro track they ran announced that the entire show would be dedicated to the book *Chariots of the Gods?!*

Nova?!

Chariots of the Gods?

NOVA!!

CHARIOTS OF THE FUCKING GODS?!

ERIC VON FUCKING DÄNIKEN?!

I hadn't been so shocked since Mary Jo Bingham told me she might be pregnant. Her mom later explained that you can't get pregnant from kissing but for the rest of third grade I steered clear of Mary Jo!

After picking myself up off the living room

floor, slapping myself in the face and checking that I hadn't accidentally ingested any hallucinogenics, I honed in on the show.

The good folks at PBS systematically, chronologically and in articulate detail presented all of E.v.D.'s major theories, backed up by the 'evidence' contained in his, cough, cough, 'book'. Approximately fifty minutes of the Plains of Nazca, the Pyramids at Giza and the Sarcophagus of Palenque and how they all showed definitive proof of alien intelligent intervention and design. All here on good old Terra firma.

Hypnotic and slack-jawed I sat.

Now, when I die I will likely have to spend some time in *Nova* purgatory, and rightfully so, because I didn't give the boys in the studio's writing room enough credit because then came the last eight or ten minutes of the program. In the vernacular, they essentially tore him a new asshole.

In a live interview conducted by *NOVA* Thor Heyerdahl denied ever hearing of E.v.D., much less meeting him and descending into the caves of South American with E.v.D. at his side as detailed in the 'cough, cough' book.

A local native South American sculptor, who NOVA found and interviewed, described in detail how von Däniken paid said Peruvian native more than the going rate to carve a space man sitting at the controls of a ship which he then rubbed with donkey dung to simulate aging.

Similar carved stones were found in a nearby museum, just a stone's throw away. (Sorry, had to do it.)

100

Finally redemption came. They confronted von Däniken in person about the inconsistencies, (the P.C. epidemic had just begun to infect society), of what he had published and what they had discovered.

He obviously was ambushed by NOVA and rightfully so. He hemmed and hawed for the time he was given.

I like to argue against ridiculous shit and, as the book, cough, cough, *Chariots of the Gods?* was still the talk of the town and a full transcript was available by mail.

I immediately decided that I had to have me one of them puppies!

Next day my miserly $5.00 postal money order practically walked itself to the postbox and a week later I had me a genuine, dyed-in-the-wool *NOVA* transcript.

E.v.D.'s biography was even more revealing. He had never finished secondary school, went on to fail hotel school in Switzerland and had been asked to leave a school, due to misconduct.

Now back to the overcrowded, noisy university auditorium.

Flash forward a few years to 1982 and I was in my junior year at Youngstown State. YSU was renowned for its Guest Speakers program. Big names, good money. Who should be speaking that night? E.v.D. himself in the flesh.

He was twenty minutes late, (an old theater trick - keep the crowd waiting), the lights dimmed the curtain rose and E.v.D. waddled out to the podium. All five foot two, 210 pounds of him.

101

Murmuring was prompted through the crowd by the two brown shirted Nazi-like, steroid injected thugs who took up positions flanking the podium, arms crossed in an overt signal of a challenge to anyone who might want to upgrade the lecture by throwing rotten tomatoes or starting a fight.

Flashbacks of the 1923 Beer Hall Putsch came to mind.

I was in the second row center, three meters from the podium, the *NOVA* transcript safely tucked in my breast pocket warming my little heart.

The festivities started with the Chair of the College of Science greeting everyone, maintaining the sense of academic decorum by glancing up to the students in the rafters, and talking briefly about E.v.D.

Finally he introduced the man and, like a slowly spreading, contagious rash, a feigned semi-enthusiastic applause broke out.

He kicked it off with a quote from that most factual source of all sources. That edifice of scientific learning and authority which had given mankind and civilization so many progressive lessons in the past - *The Holy Bible*.

Referencing *The Book of Ezekiel* and the burning bush to reinforce his point, he retreated to the overhead projector where he showed some slides of how the burning bush was actually a space craft.

The highly anticipated floor show began to deteriorate about twenty minutes into the show when he apparently realized it had slipped his fragile mind he was speaking to a room full of actual scientifically literate experts.

Maintaining an air of professionalism was difficult as he presented further 'proof' that, by the laws of physics, it would have been impossible for the ancient Egyptians to have moved those 6 to 10 ton stones on their own.

A graduate student from Dr. Feinmann's physics department quickly interjected from the back of the room, that some of the slabs at Stonehenge were five times the weight of the blocks of Giza and besides the modern Egyptians had already figured out how the Giza stones had been maneuvered into place.

This opened the flood gates.

Accusations and challenges flew.

Now, it is widely accepted that lies and fabrications in law, business, politics and religion are part and parcel of doing business. There's a whole, extremely lucrative profession based on these deceptive practices. Its practitioners are called 'lawyers'.

In science, as Charles Dawson, alias the Piltdown Man fraudster and others found out the hard way, there's no room for that shit in the sciences.

After ten to fifteen minutes more, which Jerry Springer, Oprah and Dr. Phil would have been envious of, Eric had had enough. With a quick mumble to the effect he would return in twenty minutes to answer questions, he boogied out stage left.

I moved to the aisle and as E.v.D. sped past me, the Arnold Schwarzenegger wanna-be body guards in tow, I yelled at him in German.

"Mr. von Däniken! Mr. von Däniken! Have you any comments on *NOVA*'s exposé about you?"

Talk about how not to win friends and influence people!

The Russians halt on the Nazi advance on Moscow was probably less dramatic then von Däniken stopping in his tracks causing his Gestapo bodyguard to crash into him. He turned and yelled back in German.

"Who said that?!" Several observers later reported they actually saw his left eyeball leaking blood.

My last karate lesson flashed through my mind as the Three Horsemen turned and approached me.

They stopped a few feet short of where I stood but he inched forward and looked up as my five foot seven frame towered over him and he demanded to know who I was and what my problem was.

Continuing in German to force a response, I pointed out that 100% of all of his 'proof' was falsified and asked him what his motivation was for such an elaborate charade.

He yelled back about his 'proof' and one of the goons moved to step between us which I took as a sure sign that this scene was a repeat of others at previous shows.

As I saw his head about to detonate like Fat Man over Nagasaki, I had to step back a bit. He fumbled for an answer which never came so, instead, I asked him for an autograph. He pulled a pen from his pocket and I thrust the NOVA transcript out. As it was face down and the blue paper jacket was devoid of any print he likely never knew what it was as he begrudgingly parted with his miserly little scribble which I assumed was his name. He and his entourage-ette stormed out of the auditorium and I was immediately flooded with bystanders wanting to know what was said.

I was later told that he was threatened with non-payment for the gig if he didn't return to the podium, which he did nearly an hour later where upon he danced around two questions and then left the place as if it were on fire. Which, in a sense it was.

I read in the papers a couple of days later that the rest of his Midwest tour had been canceled. I was very happy to have put a dent in his dishonestly earned but legitimately acquired fortune.

To this day whenever I'm struggling to get a novel published and more importantly promoted, I remind myself of Eric von D's sleazy, ridiculously shameful but financially successful efforts at reaching No. One and maintaining his best-selling status. Not that I'm ever tempted to give into the Dark Side, but I can't help but wonder how many others in the publishing industry have.

I also learned that no matter how bad something is, with enough promotion, people will buy it. Witness von Däniken's net worth.

Such despicable behavior is not surprising, after all some people are still putting pineapple on pizza.

Which reminds me of the time I was working late one night out in Hollyweed in a script editing house and ordered a pizza form Chico's Pizza and was delivered a box of white bread slices with

105

melted, yellow American Cheese Food topped with tomato ketchup. To Chico's credit they had the common decency to cut the crust off the bread.

But that's another story.

THE END

ON ORIGINALITY
(First published in June, 2014)

There is a growing opinion that there appears less and less creativity in the film and music industries, an opinion to which I subscribe.

I put it down to interruptions and anxiety, a loss of the ability to focus on task. You can't create when you're constantly being disturbed. You can't be creative unless you're relaxed and focused. Interruptions and anxiety kill creativity.

Pressure to produce always has and always will disrupt, distort or destroy the creative process.

Tangled up in this cycle the artist, especially those driven by fame, often revert to out and out plagiarism. It's not justified but that's what happens.

The damages to the would-be-artist once plagiarism is exposed aside, there exists the extremely detrimental knock-on effect of messaging young artists that 'copying' another's creations is the same as being 'influenced' by those same works and so it's okay to copy. Much like Tarantino's endless abuse of the word 'homage'.

Copying is not the same as being 'influenced' by and is certainly not paying 'homage' to another.

It's not okay to copy.

There is a clear difference between being influenced by others and their artistic achievements and replicating and or plagiarizing their work and trying to pass it off as your own.

If one cannot see these clear differences then

they are best advised to return to the drawing board and start over or consider another way to pay the rent.

The few simpletons who argue, there is nothing original in the world, the 'everything has been doners', should be arrested, tried and convicted with a sentence of being forced to learn new languages and travel the world for a minimum of five years or more. At their own expense.

Upon their return and before they are allowed to crawl back into their caves, they must produce some original work of anything. Failing to do so should result in an additional punishment whereby they are forced to listen to 24 consecutive hours of Lady Gaga, Mila Cyris or any boy band while watching all the Tarantino movies back-to-back without interruption on a continuous loop.

Okay, maybe not **all** Tarantino's movies, that is a little extreme and could be construed as cruel and unusual. But you get the point.

How do you explain to such idiots how it was that somebody had to be the first to deny the existence of a god, even before Nietze? *Circ de Solé* didn't exist until somebody did it. *2001: A Space Odyssey* didn't happen until Kubrick had an "OH SHIT!" moment and Electronic & Techno music weren't even words when the guys who would become Kraftwerk composed and released *Tone Float* in 1969.

And let us not forget to pay homage to the first man to eat an oyster. That guy may have been starving but he was pretty god damned original too, at least, in my eyes. Oh yeah, and brave to boot.

"Grog, eat this big, slimy booger I found inside this hard, white chalky shell thingy and let me know how it tastes."

SLURRRPPP! Grog - hero.

I'd be willing to bet nobody fucked with Grog after that day. They either thought he was hung like a bull or bat shit crazy. He probably went on to invent the first bow and arrow, the wheel, discovered flint or something else pretty significant.

For me the first observation of the unbridled lust for fame and money in The Arts came in the form of an exceptionally lame attempt to mask the blatant plagiarism of music and melodies of others. This was ludicrously labelled, "Sampling" by talentless hacks and their managers in the 80's.

These pathetic losers, who could not even be labelled rappers, spewed meaningless garbage into a microphone over the top of stolen melodies or intros licensed to others and for a short period brought the commercial music industry to a new record breaking low on the Brian Epstein scale. They were apparently so stupid, (ignorant is too gentle a word), they didn't even know such things as licensing laws existed, at least that was by and large, their story when legitimate talents started going after them and dragged them into court.

Unfortunately the practice still persists with some of the less talented rappers & pop people, but at least the plethora of lawsuits sparked by the bootleg aspect of this weak practice has forced those who still use it as a crutch, to pay royalties.

Another regrettable aspect of blatant plagiarism in the music industry is that it apparently has no racial, financial or political bounds. Witness Ray Parker Jr's rip off of Huey Lewis' *I Want A New Drug* which became the *Ghostbusters'* theme. Ray no doubt has since realized that if you are going to plagiarize music you should do 'it from someone who is not so famous, a song that is not already a hit and from a guy who can't afford a room full of Jewish lawyers to go after you.

George Harrison's so called 'unconscious' use of The Chiffons' 60's hit *He's So Fine* given a not so convincing make over to become *My Sweet Lord* landed Harrison in court in 1976 and launched the litigation trial of the century which dragged on until 1998. As a result of the inordinate amount of suits for plagiarism in the music industry and spurred on by the Harrison case, plagiarism laws have been revamped to expedite speedy settlements to limit damages to the litigants as well as the court system.

However the American courts, as is often the case are still amazingly inconsistent on the rulings of Sampling law suits.

As can easily be surmised, the music industry is not alone in suffering blatant plagiarism in the head long pursuit of fame, glory and riches.

By far the most revolting attempts at artistic rip-offs are in the film industry, logical one might argue as it is here the greatest financial gain is to be realized.

The very talented actor and comic Eddie Murphy and his side kick Arsenio Hall along with Paramount Pictures were publicly and financially spanked in 1990 after their release of the film *Coming To America* in 1988 a lift of Art

Buchwald's original 1982 script treatment for Paramount.

Tarantino's rape of the word 'Homage',(q.v.), immediately springs to mind here. He was, according to himself, paying 'homage' to the 1950's drive-in B films when he made *Grindhouse* in 2007. In reality he just took a half dozen movies whose copy write had run out and melded them into a three hour shit fest.

The colors used in lieu of robber's names in *Reservoir Dogs*, as well as several other plot points, are snatched from *The Taking of Pelham 1,2,3* with Walter Matheau and *Pulp Fiction* was a compilation of gangster stories gleaned from others and manipulated into a short story montage and re-edited. Large parts of his dialogue in the script stick out like sore thumbs as they are written with painful repetition or the trite use of clichés.

The thing that gets up my nose the most is not just that he's a master plagiarist, but that so many young people have come to believe him so prolific through his "originality".

I was once single-handedly responsible for the demise of an *Inglorious Basterds* party when, in the course of a conversation concerning how original Tarantino isn't, I informed the dozen or so young ones that the film was a remake of the 1978 feature *Quel Maledetto Treno Blindato* by Enzo Castellari. My drink was nearly knocked over by the wind of the deflated egos.

I was recently told by a fellow journalist that Tarantino has finally started admitting that his stuff is primarily lifts and remakes. Fair play to him if the report is true.

Back in the late Sixties it was common for writers to mail scripts to film companies or people the writer believed may get the script into the right hands. This is not longer allowed.

In one case a script received by producers was refused and, in spite of this, a couple of years later a film was produced and distributed. The producers immediately got the pants sued off of them for far more than it would have cost to pay the writer for the script. DEW!

This essentially led to film companies refusing to read unsolicited scripts, which they used to do. Nowadays most companies file unsolicited scripts unopened straight into the circular file. The producer's actions of course caused irreparable damage to freelance writer's getting picked up by independents and smaller companies.

Another case, which is apparently still not settled, involves the mega hit *Matrix*. However in attempting to get the facts of this case another more sinister problem arises; the false news and fabricated stories contaminating the net. From Google to Facebook the 'true' or factual story of this suit, (or nonsuit), is impossible to discern.

Some sites claim there was a suit and a settlement, others claim there was a suit but no settlement and others claim the entire story was fabricated.

This brings us to another recent anomaly in film, the endless prequels, remakes and sequels. *Rocky 7*? You're shittin' me! Nope. *Die Hard 5*! I love Bruce, but . . . surely there must be work out

112

there for a middle-aged action hero who's pretty good at comedy and drama as well? If not, Bruce let me know and I will gladly pen something for you.

Once one comes to realize that film in America is essentially about the bottom line, the production track which is easiest to predict is the video game "spin off".

Now, just in case you're one of those idiots I mentioned at the top of this piece and believe everything's been done, allow me to introduce one of the more original scams of plagiarism, what I have christened the *DaVinci Code* double scam. Stay with me on this one because it's just convoluted enough to glean a John LeCarre script from.

A guy, Mr. Brown, (no really, Dan Brown), writes a, for lack of a better word, 'novel'. Through it hundreds of thousands is invested in promo. It gets picked up. However, it's been a long time since the publishers had had a mega hit. Plus they, the publishers, or perpetrator #1, have been getting their brains beat out, along with the rest of the publishing industry, by the computer companies who have hit on the original idea of eliminating, what they believe to be, **two** of the useless middle men in book publishing. The publisher and the writer.

Well the writer's not eliminated altogether, he just doesn't get paid after he's submitted his work and it's published unless he yells and screams enough. But that's another script or a 'sequel' if you will. Working title? *Amazon Publications: The Sequel.*

To offset the damage of the surprise electronic

113

revolution/coup de tat and ensure a mega hit in Mr. Brown's book, more money than has gone to support the War in Afghanistan is pumped into P.R., promotion and propagation of the myth that this book will be the greatest hit since the Bible. And guess what? People buy it. The book and the bullshit.

Normal course of action you say? Okay, it gets better.

Daughter of God by Lewis Perdue published three years before Brown's book also sought a suit against *The DaVinci Code* after its release but, apparently with Doubleday's, (publisher), deep pockets was successfully counter sued.

Michael Baigent, Henry Lincoln and Richard Leigh writing for Johnathan Cape as publisher back in 1982, wrote *The Holy Blood and The Holy Grail* also brought suit. This, along with Brown's damaging insistence that his 'facts' in the *The DaVinci Code* are completely factual and historically based when virtually every educated historian on the planet is able to show he has fabricated fantasy and fiction into fact, haven't damaged his reputation largely because he is now too valuable a commodity for the publishers to let slip into oblivion. By continuing to pump tens of thousands into promotions, Brown is able to remain in the public eye.

In reality, with the exception of the characters' names in Brown's book, nothing is factual.

I wonder if he ever met Eric Van Däniken?

Is it that the system, like the National Lottery, promises the chance of untold millions if you can just design the right scam?

Slyly there was no hardback of *The DaVinci Code* released, initially. Suddenly, after all this time on the stands, in book shops and online, a law suit appears. "PLAGERISM!" the carefully cancelled plaintiff cries. As headlines reach an all-time high, low and behold – a hardback appears. On the back of the high profile law suit case, sales sky rocket!

Oh say it ain't so Joe!

After weeks back on the Hard Back Best Seller list, sales begin to fade. But that's okay, because the actual book Brown was accused of plagiarising, *Daughter of God*, is re-released, so the public can decide.

With more promo it climbs the charts. After a few more weeks of legal wrangling, suddenly, in New York District court, the parties kiss and make up.

Sweaty palms connect, lawyers convene, papers are signed and more money than went into the entire Apollo space programme is splashed out on P.R., promotion and propagation of the myth that this film, *The DaVinci Code*, is greater than *The Bible*. The movie or the book.

"Hello? Mr. Warner? I got a sure fire idea for a hit script! I'm talkin' through the roof!!"

"Absorb influence. Exude originality."

THE END

WOMEN

(First published in June, 2015)

The new movement which some have labeled Third Wave Feminism bothers me. Milo Yiannopolous, the British journalist, argues of the damage it is doing to the male-female relationship as do a number of reformed feminists. And he should know. He's overtly gay.

Others argue the various aspects of feminism in general. As the ages old war between the sexes continues, and having lived through a divorce, (btw, if you think you've earned your battle badge at some stage and haven't yet been subjected to a journey through the excitement which is a modern day divorce, you haven't lived).

However, in its defense I must say that the new 'modified' or de-radicalized feminism is encouraging. The women espousing this approach seem to be educated and have both feet on the ground.

I have devoted long tedious hours of intense contemplation to the conundrum of the battle of the sexes and have arrived at the following conclusion regarding the male-female long term relationship as it applies to modern society.

I hope the following helps.

A real woman is a man's best companion. She will never stand him up and never let him down. She will reassure him when he feels insecure and comfort him after a bad day. She will inspire him to do things he never thought he could do, to live without fear and forget regret.

She will enable him to express his deepest emotions and give in to his most intimate desires. She will make sure he always feels as though he's the most handsome man in the room and will enable him to be the most confident, sexy, seductive and invincible man possible.

No wait . . . sorry. I'm thinking of whiskey. It's whiskey that does all that shit.

Never mind.

My mistake.

THE END

117

MAN VERSUS MACHINE
Or
MOVE OVER JOHN HENRY
(First published in June, 2016)

It was April of 1972 at the Naval Air Station in Lakehurst, New Jersey where I had been sent to become a weather guesser, a Naval meteorologist, after the Navy discovered I had one biology class in high school and my previous six requests to go to Nam were denied.

Somebody didn't want me fighting commies.

One science was as good as another the Department of the Navy must have reasoned, so despite my three more times volunteering to go to Viet Nam to see what all the fuss was about over there, they sent me to the last place the U.S. government used hydrogen filled dirigibles, Lakehurst. That's where the Hindenburg blew up killing about five dozen and injuring nearly everyone else, an incident that was filmed and reported live via radio just as WWII was about to break out.

Happy memories.

I had been there less than a month when I was disenrolled due to misconduct and was awaiting orders when myself and another lucky eleven guys and gals, unbeknownst to ourselves, had been selected to be the first amongst U.S. Navy personnel to, voluntarily under orders, participate in a Navy experimental training program for increased proficiency in data processing and storage.

Formerly known as typing letters and filing shit.

Like rats in a lab nothing had been explained to us, an administrative oversight I'm sure because the Navy always took great pains to explain to us in fine detail everything to be accomplished so that we would always be as prepared as possible for any conflict or situation we might encounter. Just like in WWI, WWII, Korea, Viet Nam, Iraq, Afghanistan and insert next conflict here, _____.

So we filed into the small classroom where all 12 desks were armed with what appeared to be props from the latest *Star Trek* episode.

As I sat for the first time in front of my very own huge, green faced monster, the size of a Motorola console television set, which I had earlier seen being uncrated and carried into the classroom by two large and husky delivery guys, I had to remind myself that I was under orders from my commanding officer. This looked dangerous.

In reality there were about 18 desks crammed up against each other in the cramped room which became even more crowded with us, but due to the size of the HAL 3000's, which loomed before us, each occupying one and a half desks, we could only get at 12 of them. At least we had ample elbow room. A fact I failed to appreciate because of the distance it put between me and the cute little, blond corpswave next to me.

Green eyes! SHIT! Why'd she have to have green eyes?!

After an eerie fifteen minutes staring at the boldly printed signs taped to the machines:

"DO NOT TOUCH MACHINES UNTIL TOLD TO DO SO!"

our clog clad class instructor clopped into the classroom.

Sadly she was a mere glimmer of Miss Marie Watonoyski my five foot, ten inch svelte, green eyed, blond typing teacher from which I had sorrowfully departed following high school graduation less than six months earlier. Did I mention she had green eyes?

I never understood why Miss Watonoyski never responded to my telepathic messages of love and sexual desire for her. From the first day I stepped into her classroom I knew she needed me, she just hadn't realized it yet. Probably came to her senses much too late. Poor creature.

We were then informed we would be spending one full week with Burl Ives the then still semi-known actor and voice of Sam the Snowman in the animated feature *Rudolf the Red Nosed Reindeer*. The same actor who had been black listed by crazy Joe McCarthy during the commie hysteria back in the Fifties.

The irony of being taught by a communist snowman while the Navy's war in Viet Nam raged on against the communists was kind of appealing to me. I'm a firm believer that everyone has something to offer. But I always wondered why his nose was red. Rudolf's not Burl's.

As the first order of business we were introduced to a thing they called 'the floppy disc'.

Although the term 'floppy' was quickly abandoned by most of the male staff, and replaced by just the noun, 'disk', which later somehow became 'disc', the wonderment that that little black, eight inch, square disk, (oxymoron alert), could hold an entire 80kB's and still be used later to retrieve and even edit all of your saved info was a Big Brother step of significant proportions. I thought of all those poor elderly folks at Weyerhaeuser Paper Industries who would soon be unemployed. No more typing paper or onion skin. No more carbon paper and no more White Out.

Until that moment in time we had been weaned on typewriters. (Typewriters - Google it.)

First manual then only a couple of decades later, electric. Now this, whatever 'this' was. Little did we dream of what was to come.

As per Mrs. Greenbottom's instructions, (actual name), we each picked up and fondly fondled the sample disk laid out for us on our descs.

"Stand by to activate machines!" We located the green and tan toggle switch to the side smartly labeled 'ON', as instructed, and stood by.

"Activate machines!" Toggles were flicked and, one by one, across the room, scenes from the *Twilight Zone* ensued as the screens flickered to life.

An iridescent, radioactive-looking dot in the middle of the Volkswagen-sized screen glowed then slowly grew until it plastered the entire glass surface before suddenly turning a color straddling Kraft American cheese food yellow and puke, lime green. The color like when you chug five too many green apple Schnapps after four tequilas to impress a girl then run into the toilet looking for Ralph.

The glow intensified causing several sailors to slide their chairs back to a safer distance. A few instinctively covered their genital areas as the off white, Bakelite boxes eerily glowed more intensely and hummed a little more loudly.

"Insert the information disk into the slot labeled, 'Insert disk here'!"

It suddenly became clear that Mrs. Greenbottom must have had an advanced degree in word processing technology.

However, to her credit she didn't lose her cool when several of the sailors proved to be a danger to themselves and possibly to all of society. Dangerous because they had attempted to think for themselves when they tried to remove said disks from said protective casings thereby destroying said disks.

Perhaps it had dawned on her too late she should have explained that the disk would slide out of the casing once inside the football field-sized machines.

That's when I realized we weren't the first experimental batch of 'students' when I noted that the scrap basket in the corner was half full of mangled disks partially and pathetically protruding in agony from their former protective casings.

I bowed my head and said a quiet prayer to the Circuit Gods hoping that the floppy little fellas had led long, productive lives before their untimely demise at the hands of less astute sailors who were probably boatswains mates.

Now the numerous clicks and buzzes spewing forth from the machines in front of us, post disk insertion, clearly indicated what had become of Robbie the Robert form *Lost In Space*. Some evil genius had shrunk him down and imprisoned him inside this IBM plastic prison.

Evil knows no bounds. I knew it was Robbie because he was clearly signaling for help to escape.

"Click-click-click, buz-buzz-buzz, click-click-click!"

As frustratingly impressive as the situation was I didn't speak binary and so focused on attempting to read the Morse code message now being silently broadcast by the flashing, green square dot in the upper left hand corner of my glowing, apparently radioactive screen.

Square dot? Sqot? Squat? Whatever it was it was flashing away.

'Dot - dot - dot!' or was it 'Dot-dot-dot-dot-dot'? Was it signaling the letter 'S' or the number '5'? I couldn't tell. Maybe neither! My brain screamed. *MY GOD! ITS GOT A PULSE!*

"Type your name." Came the next instruction. I obeyed and my name dashed onto the screen in slow motion from where the sqot used to be. The spry little sqot now pulsated at the end of my name.

As the little blond next to me gradually sent me clandestine signals of interest by continuing to ignore me, we continued taking instructions from Mrs. Greenbottom for the next hour and half when we were told to don the headphones hanging under our desk tops.

Mechanically we obeyed the high priestess of technology and the amicable voice of big Burl Ives introduced itself and then took over the increasingly

123

complicated instructions which we would, for better or worse, richer or poorer, in sickness or in health, carry with us for the rest of natural lives. Kind'a like Herpes.

Finally it was time for lunch.

It was my patriotic duty to invite the little blond to lunch. Unfortunately my patriarchal benevolence was shunned with some lame excuse about being engaged or something like that. Accepting the fact that she was obviously a lesbian, I dined alone.

Returning from chow that afternoon, due to the fact that the temperature in the room had, through the morning, reached that of the surface of the sun we were told we could remove our now sweat soaked jackets.

Seized by a sudden, irresistible fit of reckless eyeballing, my hazel blues drifted over to the little blond as she artistically slid her jacket off in slow motion with the grace of a Russian ballerina dancing the introductory movement of *Swan Lake*.

It was at that point that I knew she needed me and it was only matter of time before she would come to realize it. I vowed to save her from herself by marrying her.

Our children would be both intelligent and beautiful!

Finally, at the end of five continuous days of being hooked up to a machine, without benefit of having been in a crippling car accident requiring life support, we had learned how to write a letter using the first prototype, desktop computers.

My money was still on typewriters, but I knew, in time, I would be out gunned by the boys at IBM and our daily existence would come to be dominated by technology. Electronic gadgets, it had been discovered were just too profitable and cheap to produce to be gathering dust on a laboratory shelf. Especially when you were under no obligation to guarantee how well they'd work or how long they'd last.

I haven't seen *Rudolf the Red Nosed Reindeer* or the cute little blond since but I did realize, by the end of that week that, along with the Twentieth Century, the Buck Rogers technology our fathers had been promised back in the Thirties had finally arrived.

Still waiting on those fucking flying cars though!

THE END

THANKSGIVING IN ATHENS, GEORGIA

(First published in June, 2016)

I spent a month in Athens, Georgia one weekend.

A buddy I wrote a medical discharge for to get him out of the Navy back in 1974 while we were in Uncle Sam's Yacht Club together, and whom I hadn't heard from since pints were cheap, contacted me out of the blue with an invite up to his place for Thanksgiving.

The balmy, sometimes scorching heat, mosquitoes and old people of Jacksonville, Florida where I lived was not the ambiance I remembered suitable for the Autumn and Winter holidays so, not realizing Georgia was but a suburb of Florida and the weather wasn't much more amenable, I accepted and we firmed up plans.

Having never seen or been exposed to the stereotypical 'Southern Fried Rock', hillbilly, trailer, shot gun rack in the back of the pick-up truck, cousin marrying environs I welcomed the opportunity to expand my cultural horizons. Even if only by a couple of inches.

That Wednesday I grabbed a Greyhound north, scribbled a few lines enroute and a short time later myself, two elderly blacks, a guy who looked as if he had to borrow the money for the fare and a young couple who didn't look much older than the new born they were carting around, crossed the state line into the great land of Ray Charles and peaches.

Show me the peaches!

The driver called out the stops as we cruised our way across the rolling country side.

"Aiken!"

"Augusta!"

"Anderson!"

"Alpharetta!"

"Atlanta!"

"Auburn!"

I was beginning to notice a pattern.

Finally he yelled out "Athens, last stop!" and, as I was the last one on the bus, I figured it was my stop.

I grabbed my bag, stepped off the coach out onto the three-way intersection and into the smell of diesel fuel exhaust punctuated by the sound of a pneumatic wrench screaming away in bay number one of the two bay garage at *Bo's Gas Station and General Post Office*. Gravel crunched behind me as the Greyhound, along with my only lifeline to civilization, made its getaway and got away vanishing down the two lane blacktop.

I briefly toyed with the idea of poking my head into the garage but instead took a seat on the wooden slat bench out next to the road.

Bo apparently finished removing the tractor tire he was working on as silence once again prevailed leaving the gently blowing breeze to tickle the tree tops which danced over the rolling hills in the distance.

Overwhelmed by the beauty of the changing

foliage blanketing the long, rolling hills and despite the chill of the mountain air, a warm familiar feeling crept over me. The impact of serenity on creativity was refreshed in my mind and I immediately understood the attraction the south had for some folks.

Right on time my friend, Terry alias 'Ridgerunner', a fifth generation Georgian, pulled up in his, you guessed it, fire engine red, Ford pick-em-up truck complete with gun rack.

Some stereotypes never die.

A minute later we were tooling down the road.

"This here's the Old Hull Road!" He proudly declared while lighting a hefty spliff, as if he had a hand in building the two lane hard top himself. I was further informed it ran right next to the 'soon-to-be-built' New Hull Road. An assortment of rusted and abandoned, vintage road machinery scattered along the roadside attested to his idea of 'soon'.

We drove on for a bit before we pulled off onto a single lane, macadam road which ran for a couple of miles more before turning into a dirt road which gave way to the woods where there was a dirt trail.

"We still got a ways to go but we got'sta walk from here." He cheerfully explained. I took comfort in knowing that if the Russkies picked that day to nuke us, we'd have months before the fallout reached this locale. If ever.

Sequestered in the middle of the solitude I looked around at the isolation and knew we were truly alone in this sector of God's little acre.

As we walked down the ever narrowing game trail old military habits kicked in and, as I scanned for trip wires and punji sticks, I began to orient myself by memorizing available landmarks.

To the left, trees. Straight ahead, forest. Behind and to the right, woods. Great! Got it.

As dusk began to set in and we pushed up the trail my mind wondered.

Here comes the part where three guys jump me, tie me up and say, 'Squeal like a piggy, boy!' Hopefully Burt Reynolds was in the neighborhood.

Finally we came upon a trailer in search of a park. Or one big god-damned park with only one trailer in it.

I often wondered if there's not a couple of hermit crabs on a beach near a trailer park somewhere who peek their heads out every once in a while.

"See Herb, I told you we're not the only ones that carried our homes around!"

"Thanks Doris!"

Inside the surprisingly not so spacious mobile home that never went anywhere, (no wheels; up on blocks), I found the velvet paintings were a nice touch. Dogs playing poker? Now that's just stupid! Dogs have no thumbs so they can't stack chips!

But the six plaster, hand painted Elvis statues in various theatrical poses scattered around the room didn't clash as much as I thought they would with the Merle Haggard and Johnny Cash dinner plates. However, the poster of Dolly Parton about to bust out of the frame was a bit imposing.

One man's opinion.

The overtly pregnant Mrs. Ridgerunner had cordially fixed dinner, a local favorite, chitlins, fried

129

chicken and grits. Remembering that chitlins were some kind of pig's innards, the chitlins and I quickly made friends with the pony-sized hound dog curled up under the table.

It was then after dinner, sitting at the table, that I learned a lot about this area of the country, sometimes derogatorily called 'The Deep South'.

The more we talked, the more I realized the rest of America had this part of the country all wrong.

Southerners didn't want to stay drunk on moonshine, start fights, shoot everybody and hate blacks because they were prejudice. And they weren't bitter about losing what they themselves refer to as 'the War of Northern Aggression resulting in the longest cease fire in history'.

And they weren't upset about whether it was fought over the right to cessation or slavery.

They only fired on Fort Sumter that April back in 1861 because they were pissed off at the food they had to eat.

Any food that is indistinguishable from when it goes in to when it comes out is not on my 'To Do' list.

I made a mental note to recommend a friend up in Manhattan to maybe come down there and open a couple of Italian restaurants to help these folks learn about cuisine.

Hmm. . . Chitlins pizza? Maybe not.

A long two hours later I was warmly tucked in under a pair of battleship grey, U.S. Naval hospital blankets on an Army cot stretched out in the back room. Apparently I was lucky it wasn't hunting season. That was the room they normally used to

130

dry the deer carcasses.

And here I thought the dark red floor boards were just artistically stained.

***

It was just past zero dark thirty Thursday morning when I heard the unmistakable drawl of Ridgerunner in my left ear as I felt him shaking me awake.

It was back in my early whiskey days and I was just getting used to clawing my way out of unconsciousness, so coming around in strange and foreign environs wasn't exactly a new experience but the sound of pigs rutting, a cow mooing and chickens clucking was.

"Time to go huntin'!" He gleefully informed, thrusting a rifle at me.

"Hunting?! Hunting for what, V.C.?! The war's over!"

"Squirrel! How else my wife gonna fix dinner?!"

"Squirrel! For what!?"

"For Thanksgivin' dinner! What else?! We's having squirrel stew! Yall's lucky, she only makes it couple'a times a year!"

"So she does love you!" I mumbled.

What was I thinking? It's Thanksgiving. We were in Georgia, why would we have turkey or ham for the most celebrated feast day in the United States?

Hunting squirrel was to me a bit like going out into the alley, putting down a bowl of milk and

131

when the first stray alley cat came along you'd shoot him and yell, "I got one!"

Seriously, squirrel hunting?! I had to say something.

"As far as I know the American tradition is turkey! You guys need a few bucks I'll pitch in! Come on boy! Let's get us on down to the general store and buy us a turkey!" I foolishly suggested.

"Turkey?! That's Yankee food! We don't eat nunn'a that down here! Down these parts we only eats what's we kills!"

Plurals are popular in the south.

After climbing out of my cot, cleaning up and grabbing my rifle, I resigned myself to the fact that we were going squirrel hunting. How could I have left that off my bucket lists all these years? Another first in my recently accumulating, long line of events assuring me a win the next time I played the drinking game, *Have You Never Ever?*

We set out in our cleverly camouflaged jackets and trousers. Apparently people were smarter in those days. Either that or not enough hunters had killed each other yet, but orange hadn't come into fashion when setting out to slaughter, tiny innocent, woodland creatures.

Ridgerunner knew the woods well and so knew exactly where to go to track our prey, so we headed out and walked for the better part of an hour before he declared we were in enemy territory.

As we pushed forward through the brush I looked around to stay oriented.

Trees to the left. Straight ahead, forest. Behind and to the right of us woods. Aha! Familiar territory!

I must admit I learned some valuable lessons about hunting the fearsome and wily American Grey Squirrel, known to naturalists and zoologists alike as Squirrelius Greyus Americanus.

Lessons like paying close attention to your surroundings and making a special effort when you're in a known squirrel area where there's a supply of squirrel food such as berry bushes. I also learned what to do if found face-to-face with the deadly creature.

These are some helpful hints I found to ensure your survival of what could be a potentially fatal encounter;

Identify yourself by talking calmly so the squirrel knows you are a human and not a prey animal. Stand still and slowly flap your arms to make yourself appear bigger than you are. This will help intimidate the squirrel.

Make no sudden movements. This is critical as they are known to leap literally dozens of inches and a foot or more into the air on the slightest provocation.

Also, be especially cautious if you come across a female with pups and never get between the mother and her offspring. She will attack!

If an attack is imminent, drop your pack, lie down and play dead. DO NOT attempt to fight the squirrel they have sharp teeth, claws and can pee a steady stream for up to a foot and a half.

Also avoid eye contact as they consider it a challenge and may charge blindly.

If approached by an angry male in the wild

133

avert your eyes, lower your head, turn and offer your hind side as a sign of non-aggressive intent.

DO NOT RUN! If the squirrel chases you hold your ground. Squirrels can run as fast as a race horse. DO NOT climb a tree! Squirrels can climb trees!

I once heard of a guy who while on a stroll through Central Park one balmy evening was subjected to a wild squirrel attack. Even after a year and a half of psychotherapy he was never the same. To this day he can't look at the color gray without experiencing vertigo and vomiting violently.

Squirrel attacks are rare, most of them are just curious or want to protect their food, lairs or cubs.

By the time we headed on back to the cave the next Disney picture would be minus a half a dozen of them thar little grey varmints which were stuffed in our trusty squirrel storage basket, which had the faint suspicious odor of fish.

That evening as she waddled around the cramped galley styled kitchen, more accurately waddled one step to the right then one step to the left, the incredibly pregnant Mrs. Ridgerunner seemed as happy as most people in their lives would never be. At least most people I've run across. Her happiness seemed to infect Ridgerunner who in turn beamed with overt contentment. And to her credit, the stew wasn't half bad.

I found a strange and unexpected satisfaction in my friend's contentment, something I had never known or even been aware of. I guess there's no arguing with results!

First thing I did when I got home to New York

134

for Christmas was head for Katz's Deli and order a double decker turkey sandwich with extra mustard. Hold the squirrel.

As I was laying into the three inch thick corned beef and pastrami sambo I overheard the couple in the next booth.

"I'd really like to try something different next year for the holidays." She said to her husband.

Should I tell her?

THE END

THINGS I'M GLAD I'LL NEVER LIVE TO SEE

(First published in June, 2016)

Gut instinct would tell you that you would want to see and do as much as possible before you check out and buy the farm. However, now over 60 years of age I've come to realize there are any number of things I'm damn glad I will never live to see or have to do.

I'm glad, for example, I'll not live to see the time when people will not be able to read a book.

Pshaw! You say? Well pshaw if you will but I can see *Fahrenheit 451* just up around the bend and many of the things Ray Bradbury predicted way back in 1953 already happening. And if you don't get that reference, you're probably part of the problem so put down your I-phone, sign out of Facebook and pick up your Kindle, Nook, or your Kobo device and order an Epub, PDF or, (you may have to Google this one), buy a paperback, that's P-A-P-E-R-B-A-C-K book and read it.

(Sarcastic little prick, aren't I?)

As I aged, little did I realize that more encephalon abuse was just a few floors down as the intelligence elevator began to descend more and more rapidly.

After I introduced myself as a writer to an Australian 30-something, who was staying at the hotel where I lived, he actually bragged to me that he had never read a book and never intended to.

"Wasn't no reason!" He proudly declared. This was disturbing enough, but as the conversation progressed and I looked around for the nearest exit, his rape of the English language thoroughly convincing me that he was a man of his word.

It was shortly after this that I copped on to the young people next to me and their curious quest to find an appropriate simile as they brutalized the word 'like' a hundred times or more during a five minute conversation.

Not a week later I was talking to a late twenty-something one night and she informed me that she quit reading books because there was no space between paragraphs anymore and so they became too hard to read.

A month or so prior I found myself in an argument with a 25 year old woman, reputedly college educated, who insisted that it was incorrect to indent paragraphs, and that no one did that. Dragging her into a near-by book shop I asked her to pick out any book. The look of horror on her face when she opened a novel off the shelf was matched only by the look of puzzlement on mine.

Additionally, I have no remorse about not living long enough to be tortured with endless Michael Jackson revivals. We suffered through enough of that copy-cat shit by the time the Beatles called it quits. My deepest gratitude to Yoko.

Now that Michael Jackson, like so many before him, has discovered that you can't endlessly abuse drugs, it seems we are condemned to suffer multiple "Tributes", (see 'Sampling' in former essay, *On Originality*), by the groups now on tour.

I thought it was bad enough that he was hailed as ". . .the greatest entertainer of all time!" at his funeral by some promoter. I suppose that same jackal will arise out of the slime seeking to cash in on his name in one form or another.

I'm glad that I'll not live long enough to see komputer gramer bee-koming the standard.

Two years ago at an Irish university I used to lecture in when a fellow professor called me aside in the teacher's lounge he presented me with a paper a senior undergraduate had written and handed in as her actual thesis.

"What would you do with that?!" My stunned colleague asked. He brandished a forty some odd page paper written by a student which would have been her last paper before she almost graduated. It was written entirely in text speak.

Without hesitation I said I would fail her out right, which he did.

Upon appealing her failing grade to the department, she argued that txt spk was now the standard. Fortunately it wasn't the standard at that university. She sued & thankfully lost. Had that happened in the U.S. I fear she would have won, probably on a racial, feminist or gay issue. Her supposed major? English Lit.

One of the greater blessings I'm thankful for is that I'll never live to see anything remotely classified as contemporary ChickLit stumbling and politically wedging itself into the realm of Classics. As it is we have to suffer through endless reprints and remakes at the box office of Jane Austen's *Pride and Prejudice* every 3-5 years because in the current bizarre wave of what now passes for feminism young women are told it's a classic of feminist literature.

Pride and Prejudice is a well written, well told story of 1813 English society, but there is no association whatever to modern feminism save of an example of how 'things used to be' at that time in that place.

In reality *Pride and Prejudice* can be associated with the classics or legitimate feminism as much as Oscar Wilde can be associated with gay writing, in view of the fact that, save a passage in *Dorian Gray*, he's never written one gay story in his life.

In reality one is as large a stretch as the other, and neither have anything to do with what we now call ChickLit. A more flattering term then what most people use in private.

To clarify, easy reading has its function as do simplistic, formulaic Rom-Coms. Brain candy has its place. But don't embarrass yourself by trying to shoehorn it into anything more than what it is.

If someone aspires to achieve something, anything, paint, sing, perform music or dance, compete in sport or write, then that someone, even in the deepest, darkest recesses of their mind, must accept two basic premises.

There is a right way and a wrong way to do it and there are standards. It's not a free for all. This is not up for debate any more than the fact that organized religion has seen its heyday.

There was a time not so long ago when men painted signs with handmade, squirrel hair brushes, finely, hand ground Japan colours and applied the sharpness of eye and dexterity of hand reserved for pediatric neurosurgeons. Now, with the press of a few buttons a flimsy piece of shiny vinyl is spat out of a computer, which is pasted on a window or van, the salesman collects his money and returns in six months to repeat the process after the first sign has peeled off. Meanwhile a Civil War era, hand painted pony express sign wall mural was discovered, faded but clearly readable, in the late 1960's on the side wall of a building in Lower Jersey City, New Jersey.

It's a different mentality now. The mentality of standards has all but vanished.

It's easy enough to dismiss this as nothing more than a natural progression of society, something that happens with each passing generation. But what do we do when this natural progression reaches the point when people are no longer willing to take a stance and the last traces of hand craftsmanship have vanished from civilization?

Just as language mathematics and science, craftsmanship must be preserved.

On a separate but related topic, that is quality assurance, I'm glad I'll never live long enough to see a game show host elected pres . . . SHIT! Never mind.

Finally, in the immortal words of the literary genius Stan Lee:

"Nuff said!"

THE END

WHY I PLAY THE BAGPIPES

(First published in June, 2016)

I'm frequently asked why I chose the bagpipes as the instrument I decided to devote a year's learning to and why I still lug these unwieldy things around the world with me. There are lots of reasons, but here's a few.

St, Patrick's Day with mariachis, tacos and Chi Chi Rodriquez. Being able to bitch slap uppity clergy, sex in a kilt and an overly plump bride forcibly shoe horned into too small a dress dodging piles and piles of horse shit as she marched uphill to take the sacred vows to the poor schmuck she nailed. And me on the bagpipes.

***

My ex-wife was, in her youth, a concert violist. She could sight read at speed very well which both amazed and annoyed me, mainly because I couldn't read a damn note.

It was after the tenth time that I finally bugged her into teaching me how to read and write music that she finally gave in. Sort of.

I only won the argument by threatening to withhold sex if she didn't agree to teach me. It was only months later that I realized she misunderstood and thought I threatened to HAVE sex with her that she capitulated.

What started out as a peaceful academic lesson

inside of five minutes became World War Three. Hair and skin flew and I was told in no uncertain terms that I was essentially too stupid to learn music, unable to comprehend the system and should just keep playing by ear.

Okay, maybe I exaggerate. We might have lasted about six to eight minutes.

My daughter later asked me why mommy couldn't teach me music and I explained that it was no one's fault. It was just because we were married.

A few months later, the incident mutually forgotten, or hiding under the rug not sure which, we were at the dinner table. I asked her what was generally considered the most difficult instrument in the world to play. She shrugged and said, "That's easy, the bagpipes! Everybody knows that!" I didn't know that, but now I did.

The next day I was swimming through the Yellow Pages, found a pipe master who was willing to take me on and splashed out twenty bucks for a practice chanter. The next evening a year of secret, weekly courses at twenty bucks an hour commenced.

Vindictive little prick, ain't I?

Having to work late every Wednesday evening didn't arouse suspicion because I was in the Army and my SF unit had all sorts of stuff brewing as the shit in Afghanistan was just kicking off. The NBC News informed us that the bad guys over there decided women not having the right to drive or an education and draping them in black, canvas garbage bags was the way to go and anything else was blasphemy and if violated somebody needed to have their head chopped off.

Besides that, and more importantly, they were threatening the oil!

It's not realistic to learn to play the bagpipes properly unless you can read music and so it was eleven and a half months until I had my first couple of tunes off by heart and could play them without 'catches', that is mistakes.

It was a Sunday morning when I snuck out onto the back lawn and started tooting away on a flawless rendition of *Amazing Grace*. The screen door to the porch banged open and my wife stared wide-eyed, dropping a dish in the process.

"WHEN DID YOU LEARN TO PLAY THE BAGPIPES?!" She shrieked.

"Last week!" I casually retorted. "I bought a book. These things ain't so hard. I don't know what the big deal is." Fortunately she didn't need to hear a second tune.

That was when I knew that round was mine.

Men are bastards.

REASON #2:

I'd never heard of Chi Chi Rodriguez but when I saw the fanfare and met the little fella he was a helluva nice guy and apparently a kick-ass, champion golfer.

The only time I ever played golf was as a favor to my pipe major, Jim, the guy who taught me the pipes, when I got him onto the U.S. Army course at Fort Devens, Massachusetts one Saturday afternoon.

He was a classic Scot, stood six foot three, 250

pounds and was fanatical about the game, the game he constantly reminded me, the Scots had invented. I casually mentioned one night that it was actually an Irishman, Bishop Kennedy, who originally raised the money and set up the first formalized links at St. Andrews. For some reason he cut that night's lesson short.

During the golf game at Fort Devens I was bored to tears so started drinking on the third hole and by the turn around on hole nine I was down by three strokes but feeling no pain. That afternoon when the dust settled I had beat him by one stroke.

I had hoped to take him to the club house, get him a drink and hear some really cool pipe stories. After all, he served in the British Army during the Falklands War and was the only guy to take an American pipe band to the world championships in Edinburgh and win. Ever! That's something to stick your chest out about.

Instead I had to listen to him bitch for an hour all the way home in the car about me getting drunk while golfing which is apparently disrespectful to Scotsman who consider golf a sacred, national sport.

Okay I'll give you the game involves long stiff poles, balls, holes and scoring and pulls in lots of money. But to use the word 'sport'?! Paleeese! Fucking is more of a sport than golf! It also involves long stiff poles, balls, holes and scoring but, in addition requires more focus, should last longer and is more athletic. Plus its way more fun!

Scotties, no sense of humor.

A couple of months later, when I had a dozen

tunes off enough not to embarrass myself, it happened that I had been booked for a gig the following weekend which was St. Patrick's Day. The gig was at the prestigious San Antonio blah blah club which meant you had to be in a certain income bracket to be member.

There was to be some kind of charity event in conjunction with the holiday. All holidays in Texas, to include Passover, are celebrated with tacos, jalapenos and mariachis. So like the token black guy in a Hollywood production, (usually Samuel L. Jackson), they wanted a token bag piper.

I got the call.

I took the wife, not out of guilt but because she turned heads when she dressed up. Turned heads to the point that she actually caused an accident one night in Montreal as we were out for dinner.

That's my girl!

Once at the club we were met by a very well dressed, extremely eloquent Hispanic manager in his early fifties who explained what they wanted and he ordered a drink for my wife and showed her to a table near the window.

I assembled my pipes and went upstairs to the small, second story corner balcony he asked me to play from.

There was a fantastic view of the links, the club house patio below and a fully staffed mariachi band on each side of the patio about 100 meters apart from one another.

I started with *Scotland the Brave*, to garner attention and quickly realized these peasants had never heard the pipes in their lives.

145

The mariachi music, one instrument at a time, one band at a time, slowly died away until a single guitarrón slowly strummed away. All conversation on the patio below ceased and heads looked up to the balcony.

It was mere seconds before my distinguished host reappeared at the upstairs and, masking himself in his best American P.C. disguise, fumbled with how to tell me what he wanted to convey.

"These pipes, señor. . .these pipes they are very loud, no?"

"These pipes are very loud yes, señor Cervantes. They are made for war and military use."

He politely scratched his head and surveyed the terra cotta floor.

"There is no way to play them perhaps. . .a little lower?"

"I'm sorry. Because it is an outdoor gig I left the volume control at home."

"Perhaps. . .perhaps one more song and then you may rest?"

"It'll still be the same fee."

"Oh, no problem señor! As a matter of fact, why don't you and your lovely wife stay and have dinner on us! The menu is yours!"

I could get to like this guy!

One more tune and fifteen minutes later I was back down stairs with the wife sharing two three course meals. When I asked the waiter if it was possible to get a couple of Irish whiskeys, my new best friend sent over an uncorked bottle of Jameson 18 Year Special Reserve.

It was then that I realized I could get to love this

146

guy!

Shortly after that the two hundred quid agreed upon arrived in an envelope, with a $100 tip.

It was on the way home that my wife commented. "This piping thing really pays, huh?" She said after I handed her the money as was required by law.

"Yes it do Baby! Yes it do!"

Pass the whiskey please.

REASON #3:

In the early 90's I was hired to play a wedding at a restaurant/retreat on the outskirts of Austin, Texas. The place, which was one of the few remaining Civil War era antebellum houses still intact, was perched high on a gently, slopping hill and had been completely refitted with a garden and a large gazebo at the base of the sprawling hill.

Shortly before show time the early twenty-something bride, who was apparently no stranger to a fish supper by the looks of her, came waddling down the hill in her white dress and veil to meet the wedding party gathered around a magnificent white stallion which had been snatched right from a Stan Lee Marvel superhero comic. It was down at the gazebo that everyone took up battle stations while I stood patiently up on the Brobdingnagian sized porch with enough footage to serve as a life raft for an entire Somalian village, and waited.

The idea was for her to ride the muscular white horse majestically up the hill to the music of the pipes, dismount at the porch, be received by the groom and do the vow routine. I would then pipe the happy couple into the adjoining large hall where a grand reception awaited.

Best laid plans of mice and men.

Due to unknown reasons a full dress rehearsal hadn't taken place.

The bride had never been on a horse in her life, was as tall as she was wide and to complicate things, the script called for her to ride bare back.

The horse not the bride.

Despite a stool, a step ladder and a lifting crew of four, she would make it up the ladder every time, flop belly down onto the animal's broad back and in slow motion slide back down to land on the stool. To her credit she never dropped the bouquet once and wouldn't give up.

Try and try again she couldn't mount that horse no matter how much the home team scrum got behind her. Eventually the horse's flank appeared to develop signs of friction burn and after about thirty minutes she was convinced by her entourage to accept the inevitable. Bride and horse were going up the hill, but not as one.

The only way her and that horse were going up that hill together was if she were bridled and the horse mounted her.

As the three foot wide path was lined with uneven ground on either side it was decided that, bouquet still clutched in hand, white dress and long flowing veil, the horse and bride would be led in procession by the wrangler uphill followed by the holy faithful to finally execute the dirty deed.

Her troubles weren't over. The order of march

could have been better thought out.

Through an oversight in planning the horse had been fed a hardy meal only a few hours before and had reached exactly the right stage of digestion as they stepped off. When he raised his tail to plant the first of many salami sized horse turds only steps in front of the pissed off, humiliated and incensed bride, she was battling to maintain her dignity and so was looking straight ahead. The poor girl was one step away from her day getting worse. Her delicate, feminine voice asserted itself as her dissatisfaction verbally echoed across the well-groomed grounds and stopped traffic a mile away.

"FUCK ME!" She bellowed out.

All hands to panic stations.

To further humiliate the poor girl the videographer, obviously also new at the FUBAR'ed wedding game, kept filming through the whole thing. Now he was following right behind her sidestepping the pizza-sized, slightly runny horse patties all the way up to the house, the generous trail of recycled hay and oats fertilizing the path and pointing the way.

If only Hansel and Gretel had had that steed.

It was forty minutes into the ceremony and I had yet to play a note so, in an attempt to distract them from the developing chaos now halfway up the hill, I fired up the pipes and slowly played *Oh Believe Me If All Those Endearing Young Charms*. No pun was intended.

I learned later, during the reception after the bride changed shoes, the horse procession was the groom's idea and the rip-snorting, anger spewing

149

from the bride's face throughout the ceremony sent a clear message throughout the reception;

BAD GROOM! NO BJ FOR YOU TONIGHT!

REASON #4:

Arrogance is another thing that I have little or no tolerance for. I have no use for organized religion and have nothing but contempt for the clergy, but arrogance in religious leaders is inexcusable. Never were there a more buffoon-laden collection of inbreeds who more embodied the three things I have zero tolerance for; Bullying, Stupidity and Arrogance. The three vows apparently taken by the clergy of all religions.

I was hired to direct a film I wrote for the *Gaiety School* in Dublin, Ireland. We needed a location for the wedding scene. I and a producer went over to Christ Church Cathedral to talk to somebody about using one of the smaller chapels for the scene.

We were directed to make our way back to the vestry which, if you ever get to C.C.C. in Dublin, founded in 1031 A.D., bring a lunch and a bag of bread crumbs because that's the only way you're gonna find your way back out again. The place is literally an entire city block in size with some of the original catacombs dug down into and through three or four layers of foundations. It is a sight to behold.

It must have been in one of those foundations when they were digging it up that they found the clown of a vicar we met up with and it was he who taught me that vicars somewhere in vicar school learned to look down their noses at people, literally, when they are engaged in conversation with them.

We were met by one of a small army of people milling around the back trying to look busy when the Deacon heard the magic word, 'movie' and nearly tripped over his prom dress to pop out of his corner office and sniff around.

The producer I was with patiently explained what we were looking for and that it was a student project. The Dickon, still addressing us over the bump in the middle of his long, slender, ski slope of a nose, adjusted his robes, threw back his head, held out his hand and presented his ring.

WHERE DO THESE PEOPLE COME FROM?! Are they mass produced in a factory somewhere I don't know about or is there an asshole work shop way back in the woods manned by legions of elves who assemble them by hand one at a time?

As he gradually realized we were not of his cult, he turned, floated across the cracked, marble floor and once again vanished behind closed doors. Probably to crawl back into his casket until dark.

His minion mumbled something to us about "the appropriate donation". I mumbled something to the effect of fuck off, and we split.

This was my first encounter with this genre of idiot. More would follow.

In Boston I had received a call to play at a wedding. I met the mom and the **very** young bride at the church where I could scope out the battle ground and meet the opposition. The beautiful young kid didn't look pregnant so I guessed the marriage was legit.

This church was a holdover from the 19th C.

when some people still believed they could a buy a seat in heaven and so donated prodigious amounts to that traveling road show called the Catholic Church.

As a consequence the church was as big as Yankee Stadium with Mercs and Lexis, (Lexi?), out back in the rectory's spacious parking lot all belonging to the associated clergy.

Apparently believing the wedding vows would be that much more immune to the innumerable pressures of modern marital stress, it was a big deal for these people to have the Monsignor himself do the wedding ceremony. So money changed hands, papers were signed and arrangements made.

An additional dream of this girl was to have *Amazing Grace* played at the wedding, a childhood fantasy as the mom and daughter explained to me.

Not a problem, I happily explained to them.

Not an unusual request. Millions of beautiful, young women across the globe fantasize about having a piper. Not necessarily at their weddings, just having a piper. All young women should have at least one real man once in their lives.

Well this 'priest', apparently tired of screwing up little boys' futures felt compelled to fuck up this young girl's dream wedding by loudly and firmly telling us; "There will be no *Amazing Grace* at a Catholic wedding!". End of discussion. And just in case there was a flicker of doubt he tagged the meeting with, "I forbid it!", as he threw back his Batman cape and whizzed out of the room.

(It noticed these fags are pretty good at entrances and exits.)

Still sitting at the office table after he exited, the girl was not very successfully fighting back tears, her mom was fighting back her frustration and I was fighting back my urge to follow and bitch slap the priest-a-phile.

Leaning back and glancing over the girl's back I smiled at the mom. Being about the same age, she understood this wasn't my first rodeo and nodded.

The day of the big show came and when it was near my time to perform I made my way up to the balcony in the rear of the ornate theater which offered a panoramic view of the entire, packed to the rafters venue. These folks had connections.

I looked down and scanned up to the altar and what's the first thing caught my eye?

A gilded, velvet padded, high backed throne sitting right there center stage! AN ACTUAL FUCKING THORNE! I shit you not!

The ceremony as rehearsed, personally supervised by the Holy Eminence himself of course, called for the kids, after the bride and dad did their thing while I piped them up the aisle, to kneel and listen to the frustrated game show host mumble his magic incantations to ward off the evil spirits.

Before the vows and after the march up the aisle the couple were kneeling in front of the holy man, as he smugly sat upright on his throne one foot forward, palms on the handles feigning a regal aire. They were supposed to rise with the priest, after I played *Endearing Young Charms* so they could all do the vows thing.

Earlier in the vestibule I had pulled the mom off to the side and told her to tell the kids not to get up after *Endearing Young Charms* but to remain kneeling. Mom smiled.

Wasn't her first rodeo either.

As his royal highness lifted his larger-than-life ass to get up off the throne, I finished the first number and didn't pause. I immediately broke into *Amazing Grace*.

The Kodak moment I had envisioned magically transpired.

It was one purple faced, pissed off priest who, with no alternative but to sit back down and behave right there in front of the sold out crowd silently spat and hissed as he slowly ground his perfectly manicured fingernails into the gilded angels on the handles of his throne.

Laser beams shot from his eyes up to the balcony in an attempt to disintegrate me. Luckily I had my bagpipe shields up and his evil electron beams were deflected back into the tabernacle where they harmlessly toasted the communion wafers to a light golden brown.

Sorry Jesus.

I can't swear to it but I'm pretty sure I saw a tear on her cheek when, kneeling there, the bride turned and looked up at the balcony as I decided to throw in an additional sixteen bars, no extra charge. Hell that tune's too short anyway! I winked at her and the place lit bright with her smile.

Afterwards, when it came time for dosh to change hands, the father of the bride met me back in the vestry where I was changing out of my kilt.

With no attempt to hide his artificially mustered self-righteous indignation and shallow anger he thrust the envelope at me and made some lame attempt to start chastising me. Anticipating a confrontation I cut him off at the pass.

"Keep your money. Use it to buy some dignity." I said. He turned and disappeared.

Fucking guy was as deep as puddle.

Later, as I was pulling down the drive the young groom came running up to my car and flagged me down. I stopped in the drive and lowered the window. He thanked me, presented the envelope again and smiled.

"I just want to apol-" I held my hand up.

"It's not on you." I said. "But next time she gets her heart set on something, don't let her down. You guys are a team now for however long you can make this thing last."

He smiled and nodded. He knew he was getting a BJ that night.

Despite the fact that the agreed upon fee was $150, there was 300 quid in the envelope. I smiled.

The kids had been to their first rodeo.

THE END

Also by Paddy Kelly

Operation Underworld – 2009

The American Way – 2011

Don't Eat To Live, Live To Eat -2012

The Wolves of Calabria – 2013

There's An App For That! – 2015

Politically Erect – 2016

American Rhetoric -2016

The Broad in the Kimono - 2017

Children of the Nuclear Gods – 2018

Luck & Fame Are Four Letter Words – 2018

The Galileo Project – 2019

When Two Tribes Go To War – 2022

Spicer's Circus - 2022